Also by Grace Dent

DIARY OF A CHAV
Trainers V. Tiaras
Slinging the Bling
Too Cool for School
Ibiza Nights
Fame and Fortune
Keeping It Real

Look out for . . .
Poppet's next awesome diary
in March 2010!

For Miss Lola Grace Dent

Diary of a SNOB

Poor little Rich Girl

Grace Dent

Hodder
Children's
Books

A division of Hachette Children's Books

A Catalogue record for this book is available from the British Library

ISBN-13: 978 0 340 98974 6

Typeset in New Baskerville by Avon DataSet Ltd,
Bidford-on-Avon, Warwickshire

Printed in the UK by CPI Bookmarque, Croydon, CR0 4TD

The paper and board used in this paperback by Hodder Children's Books
are natural recyclable products made from wood grown in
sustainable forests. The manufacturing processes conform to the
environmental regulations of the country of origin.

Hodder Children's Books
A division of Hachette Children's Books
338 Euston Road, London NW1 3BH
An Hachette UK Company
www.hachette.co.uk

This diary belongs to: Poppet Zanzibar
Montague-Jones

Address: The fifth-floor TV den
                  1 Octavia Square
                  London NW5

SEPTEMBER

SUNDAY 6TH SEPTEMBER

POPPET ZANZIBAR MONTAGUE-JONES'S ULTRA ENORMOUS LIST OF STUFF TO, LIKE, TOTALLY ACHIEVE IN THE YEAR AHEAD.

1. SORT OUT BOOB FIASCO.

Start nagging Mother to book me in for a boob job ASAP as I'm nearly 16 years old now and at CRISIS LEVEL in the melon department. I'm 30AA!! Actually, my ruddy nipples point inwards most of the time instead of outwards so that lady with the ice cold hands and the tape measure in Harvey Nichols just snorted at them yesterday then pointed in the direction of the woolly vest department. *Quel cow.*

Oh God, life really is so enormously unfair. It amazes me how I carry on, yet somehow I find the strength. Why don't I have an enormous set of scones like my friend Striker Earhart? Why, God, WHY? Where are my big wobbling pair of knockers that I can rest on the desk like Striker does in Maths, and make Deathbreath Douglas forget all about my algebra homework.

Action Points:
a) Email Mother's assistant Matthew and see if I can

schedule in 'face-time' with her this week when she flies in from Mustique to discuss seven grand advance on my trust fund to blow on boob job. (She'll say no. She shouted no twice on iCamera this week already.)

b) Tell my lovely best friend Vixen Diaz-Brocklehurst that she can stop her daily chanting to Buddha about the boob situation as it's just not working, is it? NO. In fact NINE WHOLE MORNINGS she's been sat cross-legged omming and nomming and clanking tiny symbols and I've still got baps like two depressed insect allergy stings on the chest of a nine-year-old boy. THANKS FOR NOTHING BUDDHA YOU NAPPY CLAD FOOL.

2. GET RID OF BRACE ON TEETH ASAP.

Holy God on high, eleven months and nineteen days is long enough to be walking around looking like this, isn't it? Like a barbed-wire fence with a joke-shop wig caught in it!

I hate this RUDDY BRACE . . . Sorry, this 'Orthodontal Correctional Retainer', as that dentist in Harley Steet called it as he sat on my chest assaulting me with PLIERS. And yes, I know, I KNOW I'll have straighter teeth in the future but NOW at this present moment I look like a cyborg, or an industrial mincing machine. In fact when Vixen, Striker and I walked past Godspeed Boys' Academy on the way to hockey last term, that pig Marmaduke Adams in Year Ten ran up to the railings shouting 'CYBORG GOB CYBORG GOB!' and THREW a baked potato at me that he'd smuggled out of the dining hall like a missile AND IT THWACKED ME ON THE HEAD, AND MASHED POTATO AND BUTTER SLID DOWN MY FOREHEAD.

The brace needs to GO. (Alternatively, I could learn to run faster and carry a squash racquet to disperse baked potatoes.)

3. SEXY-UP MY SCHOOL UNIFORM.

Now that I'm in Year Eleven I need to work out some fresh new ways to wear my Hampstead Lycée For Young Ladies uniform so that I look, like, totally MORE hot, raunchy and more importantly available for steamy full-on tongue-snogging and hands-roaming-top-half-only action with the Godspeed Academy boys just like Vixen and Striker do. I need to work out how to look LESS like that person with the face boils who comes twice weekly to collect the Tampax bins, the one we can't work out whether they're a she or a him so we call them 'Shim'.

Ideas for sexifying: fishnets under school knee-socks? Skirt rolled down, top of thong showing? Black bra under white shirt, two buttons undone? Skirt rolled up to create high waistband leaving both bum cheeks entirely viewable from behind? Oh God, I am so totally not brave enough to do this. I don't have the legs or bum either.

And being frank, what is the point in attracting boys when I don't even see the point in them anyway and I certainly DON'T KNOW what to say to them. Well aside from 'OW OW OW NOT the baked potato, OW OW OW that was my head, Marmaduke you ruddy great pig!'

4. SPEND MORE TIME AT, LIKE, STREET LEVEL AMONGST THE COMMON WORKING MAN.

Try to shake off my driver now and again and get out into the world and maybe take like, y'know, a bus. Or even one of those under-the-ground-train thingies, and LEAVE HAMPSTEAD, and really get out and meet some everyday commoner folk who wear tracksuits all the time and have jobs making things in factories and stuff. Try to experience their exciting, simple lives. Find out how to get to that Walford place where those people in that documentary series *EastEnders* live, and maybe go and meet some of them and have a 'full English' in a 'caf' with a 'paper napkin'.

Gosh, that would be really exciting. Maybe I could start with a trip to like, Kilburn High Street, which is two miles away or something. How far is that if I walk it? I never have. Two hours it would take me, maybe? Three? Must borrow some of my big brother Knute's walking boots and a good compass and a water bottle.

Must do all this in top secret, as Mother says I mustn't just wander off out of Octavia Square as it is TERRIBLY DANGEROUS. Mother says she's been out before just like, 'walking' the time my brother Knute's labrador Macbeth went missing and got picked up by a woman and taken to a council estate in Kilburn. Mother says that was a WHOLLY HATEFUL EXPERIENCE. Mother says Kilburn is full of people with terrible skin and smashed teeth who have never tasted ORGANIC GUAVA, and have never even been skiing. Mother says all the women have yellow nicotine-stained faces and wear leggings so tight you can see the outline of their hairymary, and they all get preggo by people who they don't know as they didn't switch the light on when they were doing it because they can't afford electricity, which they have to buy on a card meter because the electricity company can't trust them to pay their bills. Mother says the children in Kilburn are all on drugs and the schools you don't pay for are like WARZONES, and that's why I shouldn't just go walking off outside of Hampstead. Mother says I should use our drivers to take me places instead. Mother says the outside world is very dangerous and I need to be very careful.

She can't be right. Can she? They can't really be like that?

5. TRY TO MAKE TEACHERS AT HAMPSTEAD LYCÉE FOR YOUNG LADIES LIKE ME A LITTLE BIT MORE.

a) Try to get better grades in, like, lessons and exams and stuff.

b) Try not to get sent to the headmistress, Mrs Prendergast's, office so many times this term to, 'Repeat again to her what you've just said to me

Poppet Montague-Jones!!' And when I get there try not to say something worse and end up in even more trouble. (I seriously don't know what happens, all I try to do is be nice, it just keeps going WRONG.)

c) Try to convince Miss Babblebrook who takes Equestrian Classes that Poppet Zanzibar Montague-Jones is capable of being, like, totally SENSIBLE in charge of a pony and that it was entirely not my fault that Bramble – who is a famously naughty pony anyway – got majorly over-excited on Hampstead Heath by the sight and smell of a crowd of OAPs eating a picnic and took off galloping at eighty miles per hour, with me squealing and swearing on the back of him, before he eventually THREW ME OFF into a pile of homemade sausage-rolls and cream scones, then turned his furry pony butt around and raised his tail and pushed out a majorly enormous PLOP on to the picnic rug causing an old age pensioner to have a heart attack. DISASTER!

In fairness to myself and Bramble it was only a small heart attack. Not, like, a major tragic one or anything. The guy is fine now. He's totally walking around and talking and, like, everything. I think we all need to like, y'know, move on and stuff.

d) ~~Write a letter of, like, really massive apology to Mr Harper who takes Archery about the unfortunate incident with the crossbow.~~

e) ~~Get DADDY to write a big cheque to Mr Harper~~

~~who takes Archery to say sorry about the mishap with the crossbow.~~

f)   ASK MRS MINSK OUR HOUSEKEEPER TO KNIT A BOBBLE HAT FOR MR HARPER (PREFERABLY WITH LONG SIDES TO COVER FACE WOUND).

7. **BE MORE POPULAR AT SCHOOL.**

a)   Convince Blitzen Trapper who is the most popular girl in our year that I am, like, totally amaaaazing and HA HA-HILARIOUS, and really someone she should invite to sit with her every day at lunch, EVEN WHEN Vixen and Striker aren't there, which is when she always blanks me entirely. (No more eating lunch by myself this term on the Specialtons table, with the girl who eats lunch with a glove puppet.)

b)   Try to become really close pals with Blitzen and see if she maybe wants to come over here for 'informal supper and chillaxing' one night (even if she does always remark to me, Vixen and Striker that our houses on Octavia Square are like, totally small and pokey and we like, live like savages because we don't even have pools or tennis courts or hardly have any staff living with us).

    Important: try to be the sort of person who gets invited first to any after-school things, not just someone who tags along with Vixen as her plus one.

8. **BECOME A FAMOUS IT GIRL AROUND LONDON LIKE MY BIG SISTER KITTEN.**

a) Must try my very very best to look a lot thinner and prettier and taller and cooler so I get invited to more hot media parties, launches and film premieres just like my big sister Kitten Calypso Montague-Jones who is a legendary It girl, magazine columnist and style guru already.

b) Must get my photo taken on the red carpet by paparazzi looking really glossy and toned and amazing, while also pulling a face like it's a MAJOR DRAG for me to be there as I've really got better places to be.

Must NOT look small, fat, rosy-cheeked and really ENORMOUSLY over-excited to be there, like I did when Vixen got us tickets to the *SpongeBob Square Pants* movie premiere. Must NOT rush over to SpongeBob screaming, 'SPOOOOOOOOONGEBOB!!' and have photo taken hugging lifesized SpongeBob Square Pants doing a massive happy 'two thumbs up!' pose and a smile bigger and more demented than his.

THIS IS NOT COOL. MUST NOT DO THAT AGAIN.

Must try to get into the London *Evening Standard* newspaper's 'Top Ten Hip Young Things' list just like Vixen did last year, so that Mother will be a bit prouder of me and can ring up her best friend Pearl and BRAG about what a good mother she is. Must convince Felix

Hayes-Burlington from over the road (who Mother hopes I'll marry as he is SERIOUSLY LOADED) to attend some of these parties, so we can be, like, one of those, 'It couples' and get photographed together. Felix's mother would LOVE that too. Maybe if I do all of this my family might think I'm a bit of a, like, y'know, misfit, and they might stop taking the mickey out of me all the ruddy time and stop saying stuff that makes me feel depressed.

9. **GET ALONG MORE SMOOTHLY WITH BROTHERS AND SISTER.**
a) MUST really really try incredibly ruddy hard to get along more amicably with Knute and Flash and Kitten. NO more silly billy squabbling which totally undoes all the Zen headspace Mother is creating doing her Ashtanga yoga.

Mother says she has simply had enough of us all and THAT'S THAT. Mother says we all just have to learn to get along in this shared house with the limited space we have and make compromises. So if one of us wants to watch a movie in the basement cinema then the other one should just be calm and go and watch the 40-inch Sony Bravia in the fifth-floor TV den or the 44-inch Panasonic in the third-floor lounge. Or alternatively we should have Mrs Minsk make a log fire in the games room and hang out there, or even just take a sauna now that we've had the surround sound stereo fixed in the steam room area.

Mother says it's really not her fault that Daddy refuses

to buy us a bigger house and we all have to be tolerant of each other and not fight.

It really is hard though. Like what about when little Flash has one of his nightmares in the middle of the night and piddles in his bed and then he wanders into my room and crawls into bed with me for a hug. THEN HE PIDDLES AGAIN and I don't even realize and sleep though the alarm and don't have time to shower before school and then Blitzen smells me and sets up a Facebook group called 'WHO THINKS POPPET IS A PISSPANTS?' which gets 498 members?

HOW TOLERANT WOULD MOTHER BE ABOUT THAT, YEAH? HOW TOLERANT WOULD MOTHER BE IF SHE TURNED UP TO ONE OF HER CHARITY LUNCHES DRENCHED IN THE CONTENTS OF A SIX-YEAR-OLD'S BLADDER?

And my big brother Knute is mindbogglingly annoying too. He's always just vanishing off to, like, the South-east Asian Rainforests, to go to Climate Camp to, like, totally raise awareness about climate issues which is FINE but he leaves his stupid dog Macbeth behind at a moment's notice and Macbeth lies on his bed HOWLING AND WIMPERING for days with her head on his pillow and it's ME who has to go in and cuddle her and try to feed her chocolate buttons and maybe have a little fresh air in the garden!

And as for my big sister Kitten, well she truly is the most incredible gigantic pain in the rear end these days and I'm ruddy sick to death of her. I feel bad for writing this as Kitten and myself used to be sort of really close, like almost best friends, until recently. We had heaps of fun. BUT these days she is constantly grumpy and bitching at me, so I bitch back at her and she's always accusing me of stealing her clothes and her make-up bag and she calls me a SPOTTY LITTLE BRAT and a PATHETIC LITTLE NERD and says that I go trotting boo-hoo to Mother every time Kitten does something wrong, which sooo isn't true at all. In fact, I COVER UP FOR KITTEN SO MOTHER DOESN'T FIND OUT THE WORST STUFF. If Mother knew half the stuff Kitten is up to, well, I don't know what would happen but it would be BAD.

Kitten should ruddy realize this! Kitten should realize that if she stopped being so BEASTLY to me then I might be LESS BEASTLY to her. Maybe if Kitten stopped calling me stuff like 'TITLESS WONDER LIPSTICK THIEF', then I'll stop telling those paparazzi guys who sit on our garden wall EXACTLY WHICH NIGHTCLUB SHE IS GOING TO so they won't get such hilarious pictures of her sneaking home at 3am with used lavatory paper hanging off her shoe and her hair like a hedge and her coat on backwards looking completely OFF HER HEAD. These photos then appear in the *Sun* in the showbiz section and *Heat* magazine for everyone to laugh at.

Oh heavens. Now I read this bit back that's all actually quite serious, isn't it? Maybe Mother's right? Maybe if

Daddy just bought us a bigger house then we wouldn't have to actually, like, see each other at all.

10. **WORK OUT THE MEANING OF LIFE AND WHAT POPPET ZANZIBAR MONTAGUE-JONES SHOULD DO WITH HERSELF IN THE FUTURE.**

Wooah, yeah, like serious one I know, but I really think I should work this out *TRÈS TRÈS VITE*. I mean, I get my trust fund money in like three years' time and I think that's about, like, five million pounds or something, yeah? Maybe like, six million? I soooo don't listen properly when Mother and Daddy's accountant Mr Chenowitz invites me to his office to talk about it. I just sit there in a big leather chair that I can swirl round and round in, swinging my feet and watching the pigeons sitting on his windowsill while he drones on and on about investing thingies here and tax-free whatnot there and buying gold blah blah blah.

I'm like, 'Oh God, this is so boring because it's not like he's going to give me any of the cash now is he? NO. Mr Chenowitz says I have to wait three years and live off my monthly allowance for now. (Mr Chenowitz says for a young girl my allowance is 'much more than enough'.)

I don't ruddy understand anything about maths or money or banks anyway. I think I suffer with number dyslexia or, like, something. If you ask me what eight times eight is, I have to stop everything and shut my eyes and think for about two minutes before I come up with, like, sixty-six or whatever it is. And I only know this as Mother made me do extra maths tuition right through kindergarten and prep school. One thing I know for sure is that if I'm using my Coutts debit card to buy shoes on Hampstead High Street or something and the shopwoman says, 'No, that won't go through sorry', then I ring Daddy in New York or wherever he is and tell him and he tuts and sometimes says a rude word and then about half an hour later it works again. I also know for sure that my trust fund must be quite a lot of money because it's bigger than Vixen and Striker's funds and they both say I'm majorly lucky.

But I just find it all a major freak out frankly. Because I know that when Granny dies (not soon PLEASE GOD because I LOVE my Granny Montague so much) I'll get another pile of cash. And when my parents pop off I'll inherit like squillions more so all this money just makes me feel a bit confused inside my head and a little bit sad really as I don't really know what one is supposed to do with it.

Striker almost pees herself laughing when I say this and tells me I should stop being a complete dork worrying, and when I'm eighteen we should just go INSANE and buy an enormous three-litre bottle of Moet champagne and pour it over our heads, then buy a brand new silver Ferrari Spider and take it out on the motorway at 130mph and I should take my thong off and throw it out of the window at the police car chasing us and just go BERSERK and have tremendous amounts of fun.

And, yeah, that sounds sort of good fun but sort of scary too. Plus that would only take up about half an hour and I'd quite like to live until I'm ninety so what do I do with the rest of the time?

The thing is I keep looking at my big sister Kitten who has got her trust fund money and sometimes she doesn't look like she's having tremendous amounts of fun at all. Sometimes she looks like she's in a bit of a, well, mess. I don't think Kitten has worked out the meaning of life yet either. But that's OK because this year I'm going to work it out for both of us and then I'm going to ruddy well tell Kitten it and it's all going to be, like, totally ruddy amazing again and neither of us will be sad any more. I can just feel it.

MONDAY 7TH SEPTEMBER

9pm – my bedroom.

Today was my first day back at Hampstead Lycée, Year Eleven. It was a whole new year but to be perfectly honest it was the same old ruddy thing as ever.

When Dr Sarzberg, the family therapist, told me I should start writing things down over the next month or two so that I could remember important incidents to tell him in our sessions I said to him, 'Look HONESTLY there's, like, seriously NO point. I do the same ruddy

14

thing every day with minute amounts of variety. The only thing a diary will prove is that my life is KILL-YOURSELF-WITH-A-HAMMER dull.' Dr Sarzberg just laughed when I said that and said, 'Why don't you start with an average day anyway Poppet, as it would be helpful.'

Well OK here ruddy goes:

OK, right. I woke up at about 7am when the alarm on my Blackberry started clanging. That's when I found out I wasn't alone, as Flash was sleeping the wrong way round in my bed with a foot in my face, and Macbeth was on the floor curled up snoring in a pile of wet towels. HOW do they get in my room without me knowing? I must sleep so deeply I go into a minor coma.

Turns out Flash dreamed one of his crazy dreams again and he'd run to look for Mother but Mother had mixed up her flight times so she wasn't back from Antigua or Mustique or wherever she is (actually it may be Barbuda). And Daddy is in Manhattan all week and no one ruddy remembered to book a night-time nanny to stay over with Flash, which meant Flash had grabbed a lump of extra-strong Stilton cheese for supper and put himself to bed at 9pm watching a *Doctor Who* DVD on his laptop. Then he'd fallen asleep dreaming that a three-legged monster with a face made of snakes was chasing him to a bleak death through a haunted forest resulting in his head being waved about on a spear.

I tried to give him a big cuddle and kiss the top of his

head when he told me this but he wriggled out of my arms and walked off.

'I wasn't scared, Poppet!' he said to me as we sat at the breakfast table in the basement kitchen facing each other. Flash and I both went to bed without dinner last night so we were hoping Mrs Minsk would take pity on us and make us some breakfast, even though it's not really her job.

'Yes you were, Flash,' I said. 'You're only six. That DVD is for much bigger boys.'

Flash looked furious when I said that. Or as furious as someone three foot tall and dressed in Spider-man pyjamas can look.

'Daddy bought me that DVD!' Flash said, doing that cute thing he does where he pushes his specs up with one finger then pushes his hand through his white blond hair. 'Daddy said I am a big boy because the school says I am gifted so I can watch things for bigger boys whenever I want.'

'Really?' I said.

'Yes,' said Flash. 'That's exactly what he said. With his mouth. When only I was there.'

'I see?' I said, eating the porridge that had been put in front of me. It had honey and cream on it which was NOMNOMNOM gorgeous and totally fattening probably but I'll do some ruddy star-jumps tomorrow or something.

'He DID, Poppet,' Flash said. 'I don't tell lies.' Well

this was quite possibly a complete lie in itself. Flash tells all sorts of whoppers. That's why he sees Dr Sarzberg the therapist in the hour-long session after me.

Mother didn't appear at any point during breakfast, so I asked Mrs M when she thought Mother was supposed to be home but Mrs M was as stumped as us.

Then Karina from Hungary – Flash's favourite daytime au-pair – arrived being all cheery and floaty and ditzy wearing her long, knitted green scarf, black wool mini-dress and long brown boots and, well, she didn't have a clue where Mother was either.

Then Karina took Flash to get washed and dressed properly and walk him to school. Then one of our drivers beeped his horn outside to say he'd arrived to take me to Hampstead Lycée. So I finished my juice and took Mrs M my bowl and she said, 'Have lovely first day of term, my darling,' and gave me a little kiss and then it was time to go.

I grabbed my bag and stared at myself in the full-length hallway mirror, which Mother has just had shipped over from Tuscany. As ever I was totally EMOTIONALLY DESTROYED by what I could see. My little chubby legs hung in knee-length pale blue socks like plump Cumberland sausages. My navy pleated skirt made me look like a terminal virgin, my pale blue blouse hung limply over my ironing-board-flat chest, and my navy blue blazer with its stiff shoulders made my whole torso into a definite box shape. The worst thing was it was well past 8am already and far too late to kill myself.

I stared sadly at my mousey brown hair in limp handlebar bunches and my CHEESE GRATER MOUTH OF SATAN.

'Jesus Christ,' I muttered, then I wandered out of the door and down the steps where the Volkswagen people-carrier was waiting. Then I spotted a brown bald head and enormous wide shoulders behind the driver's seat and it made me smile for the first time that day.

'Good morning, Cyril!' I said jumping into the back seat. Cyril is really ULTRA amazing for a grown-up. He is about fifty and he comes from Nigeria originally which is, I'm pretty sure, in Africa. Cyril's voice is really deep and he can be really funny and he sometimes tells us amazing stories about how poor his life was there which are so awful that they completely NO WAY can be true and he's winding us up, but they're good stories anyway. And one day last term when he drove Flash and myself home from school and Mother was late home from a charity lunch and had locked us out of the house Cyril drove us to this place called McDonalds where you speak through your car window into a metal machine and a woman in a green shirt bought us ice creams to the window called Smartie McFlurries with lumps of coloured chocolate in them, and me and Flash and Cyril sat in the car park and ate them and a 999 police chase went past the car park when we were eating and it was the most exciting thing EVER EVER EVER! I like Cyril a lot.

'Miss Montague-Jones, good morning,' Cyril said, turning down the twenty-four hour news station he's always listening to. 'Did you have a nice summer holiday?'

'Oh it was, well, yeah, like, totally fine really,' I said trying to remember anything that I'd been doing. 'It was fairly low key to be honest. Like, we did the usual three weeks in our house in Tuscany, yeah? That sort of dragged a bit really . . . although I did a lot of painting. And Mummy had a birthday party so she had about fifty of her friends fly out there and they had this massive barbecue and she asked her favourite band The Jet Fighters to play.'

'That sounds like quite a party!' Cyril said.

'Yeah, it was OK,' I said. I tried to think of anything else that happened but my mind was sort of blank. 'Oh and I flew out to the Hamptons in Long Island with Vixen, 'cos her Aunt Miranda always takes a house there for the summer. Which was, like, cool and everything. But Miranda wouldn't really let us go anywhere alone because she thinks we're too young so we were just sunbathing and making cookies and stuff most of the time. Then we flew home and Vixen and Striker and me have just been hanging around Patisserie Blanc in Hampstead High Street drinking Frappolattes with extra strawberry syrup and eating cakes, which is why I'm so enormously fat, I guess. So, yeah, nothing really exciting happened this summer to be honest.'

Cyril laughed at this. Cyril finds lots of things I tell him amusing which is weird because most of the time I'm not trying to be funny at all and I'm mostly just rather dull. I think he's maybe being kind because he knows I'm a bit of a dork.

'What have *you* been doing?' I said.

'Oh you know me, Miss M-J,' he said setting the engine off and driving around the square. 'Just driving here and driving there. Keeping myself out of trouble.'

I waited for him to say something else but he didn't. He must have been keeping something secret because he can't have just been working every single day for seven weeks can he? Surely everyone goes somewhere in the summer? Takes a house abroad somewhere or something?

'So, right, it's the school run today?' Cyril said. 'We're picking up Miss Brocklehurst and Miss Earhart too?'

'Yeah,' I said. 'Let's try Miss Brocklehurst first shall we, please? Could you park up by Number 7 and just honk the horn and she'll come out.'

Cyril drove around the square and stopped outside Vixen's house and gave two sharp blasts on his horn. Within seconds the black door swung open and Vixen Blaise Diaz-Brocklehurst appeared on the steps. Cyril turned his head to stare at her like all men do then he quickly looked away and busied himself examining his sat nav instead.

'Hey, Pop!' Vixen said, waving and closing the door behind her.

I waved back, but MUCH AS I LOVE HER my heart sort of sunk just looking at her.

It pains me to say it, but this term Vixen seems to be looking even more ultra-enormously FOXY in her Hampstead Lycée uniform than EVER before. Quite aggravatingly so. She'd clearly bribed the housekeeper to take the sewing machine to her school skirt and take it up by two inches so it was just above the knee. It looked really amazing. AGAGAGAGAGH! The reason why we're forced to all buy our official Hampstead Lycée skirts from that old dusty shop Pluckfords, owned by that lezboid with nose boggles who makes you take your pants off in a cupboard then rushes in without asking, is that we're all meant to look the same!

Well let me tell you, Vixen did NOT look the same as me! She had her pale blue knee socks pulled on to her long honey brown legs with one slightly falling down as if she'd just woken up and pulled them on after an amazing all-night party. Vixen's school shirt and her blazer just seemed more neatly fitted than mine, in fact her whole shape was just longer, curvier and leaner than mine, and let me remind you I resembled a HORSE TRANSPORTATION BOX WRAPPED IN A BLANKET.

It would be easier if I could dislike Vixen Blaise Diaz-Brocklehurst and call her a cow but the fact is she is my closest friend and really the sweetest loveliest soul ever who wouldn't hurt a fly. (Even more so since she's started being a Buddhist because she's not allowed to be mean to anything so even when an enormous bitey mosquito landed on her arm when we were in Long Island she 'gently moved it away with kindness' as Buddhists are supposed to do, instead of whacking its tiny bitey head with a copy of *Vogue*, like I did, and screeching DEATH DEATH DEATH TO THE MUTANT BLOODBUG!!)

Vix opened the door and jumped into the people-carrier and pulled her seatbelt across her chest, then she looked at me and said,

'Hey, Pop . . . Wooooh my boob chanting worked! You've gone up a cup!' She was only being kind, bless her.

'Oh shut up, I totally haven't,' I said.

'Oh, Pop, you have! You never see the good about yourself do you?' she said.

'*I have a nice personality,*' I said in my best deadpan voice. Me and Vix always say that's what boys say when they mean, 'She's so fugly she makes my dangly parts freeze up like a fossil and snap off.'

'Listen, you know what I think about how you look,' Vix said. Vix says I don't realize how hot I am, which is nice, but it's also untrue. I spent a whole hour staring at myself last night and finally decided that although I have quite nice lips, eyes and nose, they are all unfortunately right in the centre of my face, a bit like a rat or a gerbil. So if I am hot, it's probably only to large, sexually desperate rodents.

'Gosh, so GLAD to be getting back to school and out of that house,' she said. 'Daddy's bringing SO much stress into that place right now. He's the one who should be chanting.'

'What's up with him?' I said.

Let me say here that I do feel sorry for Mr Brocklehurst sometimes. He lives with two daughters and his Argentinian wife and his Argentinian mother-in-law and they're all a bit hormonal and mental and space-cadety which means he usually wears the expression of a man who's just been chased for two miles through a jungle by a swarm of African killer bees. I told him this once and he laughed for a whole hour. Mr Brocklehurst doesn't laugh much so this was, like, an EPIC WIN for me.

'Oh he's moaning on about my ruddy trust fund again,' said Vixen pushing the electric window button to get air. 'And what I'm going to do with it. It's so boring.'

The thing about Vixy is she does have some quite random ideas, like last month when she announced she was going to open her own butterfly farm and breed enormous Red Admirals to repopulate the rainforests, which she would hand deliver herself. The month before there was a plan involving a pair of endangered pandas she's read about in Ho Chi Min City who Vixen was convinced would be happier living in our gated gardens in the centre of Octavia Square. Vixen called the Chinese zoo dudes herself but they were, like, all laughing right in her face and stuff saying, 'The pandas not for sale', and even if they were they weren't giving them to Vixen as you can't keep pandas on a lawn and feed them on lawn clippings and 'pony treats and crap like that', like she suggested. Then they hung-up because they were wetting themselves. Vixy is terribly sweet but she just doesn't think things through. A bit like this next thing she told me, which she said like it was the most normal sentence ever.

'Daddy has to accept,' Vixen sighed, 'that I want to save the street cats of Argentina.'

Just then Cyril let out a squawk like an asthmatic parrot, then he made it sound like he was coughing.

'Street cats?' I said calmly.

'Yeah,' she said.

'I didn't know there were any street cats in Argentina.'

'Precisely,' said Vix. 'But, like, when I was out visiting my great aunt this summer in Buenos Aires I was, like, blown away by what I saw! There's squillions of them! Poor little fluffy things with poorly paws and gammy eyes like, totally living in bushes, and going, 'Ooh help me!' and 'My tummy is empty MIAOW!' and running down back lanes fending for themselves and stuff.'

'Really?' I said.

'Really!' she said. 'It's tragic, Pop. I'm going to fly out when I'm eighteen and give them like a million pounds or two million or whatever and sponsor a mass re-homing plan and buy them all some Whiskas Kibbles. Our cat Bolshoi loves Kibbles, doesn't he?'

'When does Bolshoi get Whiskas Kibbles?' I said. 'Last

time I was at your house he was eating a grouse. That cat eats better food than I do! I had Nutella on toast last night for dinner! And the night before!'

'Oh that grouse was just a one-off!' said Vixen. 'Mummy hit that grouse with her BMW when she was driving back from the countryside so she just bunged it in the boot. That's the law, isn't it? If you kill something accidentally with your car you've got to eat it? Or something?'

'Oh I dunno, maybe?' I said. 'That's like really random isn't it? Wow. What if you hit, like, a horse? Or an enormous dog?'

'Then you've got to eat it, I think,' said Vixy. 'That's the law I guess.' Vixy and I stared at each other. We're hopeless at facts and general knowledge stuff. Cyril was really laughing now. There must have been something terribly funny on the radio.

'Anyway, I just told Daddy about the cat plan,' Vixen said. 'He's having another of his nervo breakdowns.' Vixen looked out of the window then and didn't say any more.

Just then I realized we'd nearly forgotten Striker.

'Oh, Cyril, stop here please!' I said. 'Could you blast your horn outside Number 12 really hard?'

We pulled up on the curb outside Striker's front door and sounded the horn but nothing happened. One of Striker's mother's patients, a totally miserable-looking man in a suit, arrived as we were sitting waiting and buzzed the white front door's buzzer. The door opened and he scurried down into the basement rooms where Dr Earhart does her behavioural therapy wotnot stuff.

We waited longer and bipped the horn and rang Striker's mobile which went straight to voicemail, but there was no sign of her at all. But then about five minutes later the front door swung open. All we could see was a mass of bright red hair all tangled up like a hedge and Striker's tiny body wrapped in a white towelling dressing-gown, which was slightly open at the front so one of her ENORMOUS boobs was nearly popping out.

OH MY GOD!!! Striker had dyed her hair! Like, Santa Claus red. Not ginger, not brunette, RED!

'Wow, that is like, sooo totally red,' said Vixen calmly. 'Mrs Prendergast is going to kill her and bury her in the school allotments.'

I wound down my window and started to yell (and yes I know Mother says only common people yell in the street but I was ruddy cross).

'Striker! Oh my God! Your hair!' I shouted. 'Look, it's quarter past eight, we're late already! We'll have to go!'

'Poppet!' Striker shouted back. 'This is your fault! You said you'd call me and wake me up!' Striker isn't bothered about shouting in the street. She does it all the ruddy time with her mouth wide open so you can see her tonsils.

'No, you didn't Striker, you said I SHOULDN'T call you!' I hissed. 'You said I had to stop being a boring cow and stop acting like your mother! That is what you said! I STILL HAVE THE TEXT!'

Striker tried to get her head around this but it was clear she'd just woken up a few minutes ago as her eyes were still half-glued shut and her face was all puffy like one of Mrs Minsk's cheese souffles.

'School starts in fifteen minutes!' I shouted.

'Oh just ruddy go without me. I'll make my own way there. I'll see you both in assembly,' Striker yelled. 'Just screech a bit louder in "Make Me a Channel of Thy Peace" and no one will miss me.' Then the door slammed and she was gone. I sat there with my mouth open for a moment then I closed it as my tongue was getting dusty.

'Gosh, it's warm today, isn't it?' said Vixen as if none of that had even happened. 'I hope they've got the air-con on in tutorial or we'll melt.'

'Sorry, Cyril, can we just go now, thanks?' I said. 'Miss Earhart will find her own way there.'

I give up with Striker. I really do.

We turned out of Octavia Square, down the side road towards the main road which was chockablock with rush hour traffic, then we crawled along for ages really not moving at all and I was getting jolly agitated as I knew we were going to be late, AS USUAL and Mrs Prendergast was bound to spot us running past her office on the very first day back and go all swivelly-eyed-howl-at-the-moon bonkers on us like she always does.

This would so NOT be cool. Especially after last year when we got so many letters home for 'perpetual tardiness', that Vixen's father gave the school the gift of a helipad on top of the science block just to shut the silly moo up.

'Stop that Prendergast woman haunting me about your lateness!' Vixen's father shouted as he wrote the cheque and threw it at her. The helipad was a 'gesture of goodwill', so that girls who'd spent the weekend in Europe or Scotland with their folks could at least just fly straight into the Lycée and skip the traffic jams from Heathrow and make it to school on time. In the meantime, Vixen and I still managed to be late twice a week travelling two miles in a car.

'I don't know why people get so bummed out about time,' Vixen said dreamily, pressing her cheek against the car window. 'Like, we're all on the same planetry path aren't we, Popsy? Maybe some of us are just, like, supposed to be in the slow lane.'

'Yeah,' I said as we sat at another red traffic light for what seemed like so long I could feel my hair growing.

'Maybe we're not late? Maybe the world is always early,' Vix said.

I just ignored this. Sometimes it's best to. Suddenly I had a mental idea.

'Cyril,' I said leaning forward. 'Do you think it will be

as busy as this all the way? What if Vix and myself, like, y'know, just this once, just jumped out and, erm, ran the rest of the way?'

There was a silence and then Cyril squawked with laughter.

'NO!' he said. 'Sorry, Miss M-J. I'm paid to see you through the school door.'

'Cool, yeah, I know,' I said, slumping back in my seat.

I don't know what encouraged me to ask Cyril that this morning. I'd never ever think it normally. I know how dangerous it could be if we just got out of the car and walked. There's one of those council estate places near Hampstead Lycée, which I've never ever seen, but I've heard about it and it's meant to be really dangerous. The Cottingham Estate it's called. (Well, OK, Lycée girls call it the Grotingham or the Snotingham.) Apparently the people there are, like, really ultra-violent. In fact Mother says the police won't even go there, it's like a NO GO area. Mother says even if the police do dare they need interpreters as half the people don't even speak English and the white ones that do speak English speak that half-Jamaican language that makes no sense at all.

Apparently there's a park beside the estate for people to get fresh air in but that's meant to be atrocious as people will stab you there just for looking at them and the play park is just an enormous pile of dirty druggy needles and dog turds. So many dog turds you could ski down it like the dog turd winter olympics. In fact, half the kids are infected with God knows what because they're not vaccinated for anything.

So, yeah of course we couldn't walk because we might get lost and end up there and seriously ANYTHING could happen. I don't know why I asked, I just suddenly got this weird urge to open the car door and get out and RUN. Totally bizarre. Maybe I should tell Dr Sarzberg about that?

We arrived at school TWENTY MINUTES LATE but it wasn't so bad as there was an enormous fuss going on outside the Lycée so everyone was late. It was Day One of a new term so no one had even attempted to car share so the road was jammed with Jags, Daimlers or Range Rovers and tension was ULTRA HIGH between all the parents and chauffeurs who were beeping their horns and arguing with one another. Nothing makes a Hampstead Lycée parent more angry than someone jamming the road, because they're all very busy and they all have very important jobs, or at least do important charity things, and that's why Mummy says people like us need enormous 4×4s as they need to be everywhere quicker than normal people.

To make matters worse Alessandra Sabatini from our year's mother had tried to do a three-point turn just by the front gate, which turned into an eighty-seven point turn and she'd smashed her Mercedes into Flora Bryce from Year Eight's daddy's Saab and apparently Flora's daddy had shouted, 'You stupid bitch! You shouldn't be on the road!' and Alessandra's mother was, like, boo-hooing in the middle of the road dressed in just a pink yoga leotard, tights and a headband (and you could, like, totally see her camel toe which was so YUK). She must have been on her way to the 9am class at Hampstead Yoga Village.

So then Flora's father felt bad and was trying to console Alessandra's mother by cuddling her (a bit too much to be quite frank because at one point he had both hands clasping her bum cheeks and was rubbing his body against her leg DOUBLE YAK!) Well, then Mrs Prendergast clomped out in her pinstriped trouser-suit and mega CLOMP CLOMP shoes and told them both this was, 'No way to swap insurance details', and then Alessandra's mother boo-hooed even louder. Well this was all bad for Alessandra's mother but majorly LUCKY for Vixen and myself as we could sprint through the chaos towards Room 5.1 to Notre Dame House Year Eleven's form period without getting landed with another thousand word essay entitled, 'Why a Hampstead Lycée lady is NEVER EVER late.'

We ran into class where all the usual Notre Dame girls were sat waiting. Miss Condou, our house tutor was faffing about with the register adding names with a pencil and scratching other ones off, looking generally vexed that it was September as she'd rather be back on the beach where she obviously was twenty-four hours ago judging by the state of her flaky nose.

Miss Condou's day was being made much much worse by the Right Honourable Petronella Hardy who was up in her face at the front desk saying, 'Will you be saying our titles this year when you take the register, miss? Will you call me the Right Honourable Petronella? Will you?' and, 'What is the point of me being a Right Honourable if you don't say it every day, miss?' and 'My daddy says he wants you to say my title, miss!' And as usual Bettina and Livvy were telling Petronella to sit down and shut her mouth as she's always quacking on about being a Right Honourable, while poor Iris Stanmore-Smyth never says a word about what we should call her and she's actually Lady Iris because her daddy is an Earl.

And then someone brought up again that 'Poppet is eighty-seventh in line to the British throne and she doesn't even tell anyone!! In fact if there was like a bomb at a royal wedding or something and loads of royals died then Poppet could be Queen!', which is true but I don't ruddy care and people can call me whatever, I DON'T CARE, and honest to God we've been having this argument since Year Seven and it never gets any more interestingzzzzzz ENORMO-YAWN to the power of a million.

Vixen had sat down at the back of class beside Blitzen Trapper. I shivered a bit when I saw that. I'd never ever just plonk myself down next to Blitzen. In fact I never know where to sit full stop when I walk into class and I always dawdle and look around for a while feeling silly as everyone has their territory and the territories sort of shift day by day and it gets sort of confusing. But Vix never notices that sort of vibes and territory thing. Vix just sits wherever she wants and no one ever challenges her. It's like she's got some sort of golden halo shining above her head. Everyone likes her. Even Blitzen Trapper looked happy to see Vixen, and Blitzen can be, like, ultra random in her moods. (Not that I'm slagging Blitzen, I like Blitzen if anyone finds this and reads this.)

Blitzen looked quite different today to how she did last term. She'd had her honey blonde bobbed hair dyed white blonde and cut short into an elfin style. She had curled up the front into a delicate quiff and squirted it with something rock hard. It really suited her slate grey eyes and her cheekbones. She looked like a pixie. Just not, like, a good pixie that does good deeds or helps people or anything like that.

Blitzen was sitting with her two BFFs, Belle Caribou and Amelia Strang, and they were leafing through *Grazia* and discussing things they wanted to order from the spring/summer collections. When Vixen walked over they all started making a huge fuss of Vix telling her how AMAZING she looked. Had she been to a spa in Thailand or something? Which one? Had she had the hot stone treatment because her skin was glowing!?

None of them said much to me at all.

Amelia sort of looked at me oddly when I walked up. When I tried to sit down she tossed her jet black ringlets and said, 'Not there, move one along, I'm saving a seat just in case.'

I looked at Vixen to back me up but she didn't hear as she was too busy chatting. I sighed then moved to the end of the bench and sat down.

'Oh my gosh, Vixy look at you, you've lost so much weight?' Blitzen said. 'You look AMAZING! Have you been detoxing?'

'Oh no, not at all,' Vixen said. 'I was in Argentina for a bit and I caught a stomach bug. I was on the loo for a week. It was gross.'

'Oh amaaaaazing,' said Blitzen, 'you're so lucky. I've had to sweat off every pound! I jogged six miles every single day and I did that master cleanse detox. The one where you just drink syrup water with molasses in and you keep fainting? I've been majorly strict with myself this summer.' Blitzen held out her right arm for us all to admire. Everyone gasped. It was basically just a bone with a thin covering of skin on it. It looked quite freaky really but I was totally jealous all the same. My arm is sort of soft with a little bit of fat at the top. Amelia calls girls who have those type of arms Bingo Wing Mingers so I always keep my cardigan on even when it is hot.

'I'm six stone eight pounds!' Blitzen said suddenly.

'Wow!' said Belle, pinching Blitzen's arm. There was nothing to pinch.

'Six stone eight?!' said Vixen. 'Crikey! I'm not that slim Blitz. I'm like, seven-and-a-half stone!'

Amelia and Belle both nodded and said, 'Me too.' I joined in and mumbled 'Me too' but my cheeks felt hot and I hoped no one could see because then they'd know that I'm not that thin at all.

The room went quiet then as Miss Condou started talking and all the girls were secretly checking their Blackberries and iPhones inside their bags for messages. I sat staring out of the window at a crowd of pigeons on the the hockey pitch feeling hot and silly and a tad cross. My brain kept thinking about Blitzen's diet. Six stone eight? Blitzen is about five foot seven! I'm nine stone three and I'm five foot five! How can I be that freakishly heavy? NINE STONE THREE? How? How, no matter how hard I try to eat boring sensible stuff like fruit and run around the gardens and take Macbeth for walks and stuff, how am I still this big?! And why does mother's dietician Mr Singhpal who she sent me to on Harley Street keep saying that nine stone three is the normal healthy weight for a five foot five inches tall teenage girl?

Why?!

Why does he say that I have curves in the right places and I'm totally healthy and NOT fat if I'm NOT the right weight at all, I'm NINE STONE THREE! Tons fatter than every other girl who ever mentions her weight ever and THIRTY-TWO pounds fatter than Blitzen Trapper! How? The doctor must be LYING to me like grown-ups always do.

Well, just as I was in the middle of a major internal chunter, the door flung open and Striker ran in and then things really kicked off because Miss Condou saw her hair which close-up looked even more OH MY GOD MY HEAD IS ON FIRE RED and Striker didn't even manage to get one butt cheek on to a chair before Miss Condou screamed 'AAAAAAAAAAAAAAIE! GET TO MRS PRENDERGAST'S OFFICE NOW, STRIKER EARHART, YOU KNOW THE SCHOOL RULES!'

And Striker said, 'Oh God, I'm only forty-five minutes late, I've not even missed start of term assembly.'

And then Miss Condou began visibly shaking, which she really shouldn't have as her nose was flaking off in clumps and falling into Iris's pencil case and she yelled, 'Not the lateness, YOUR HAIR! And, well, OK yes, the lateness too! But mostly YOUR HAIR, IT IS A MONSTROSITY.' Then Miss Condou stormed to the back and grabbed Striker by the arm and started to drag her out of the classroom and Striker said, 'Don't bloody touch me, I'll sue you.'

Well the class started giggling now as we all know that's what the scummy kids down at the Snotingham say and at Hampstead Lycée the teachers can do what they want. So Striker was wiggling and trying to get out of Miss Condou's grip and then she turned around to me as she went and said, 'Jesus, Poppet, I don't know why I bothered getting dressed, I should have just texted them a photo then had a lie-in. See you later, baby.'

'I'll come and find you at break, right?' I said, rolling my eyes.

Then Miss Condou got even angrier and screamed, 'Striker will be at home! She's going home!'

And Striker hooted loudly then and said 'AMAZING.' And then she was gone.

Striker has been suspended for a week from Hampstead Lycée and only allowed back on the condition she wears a hat. To be quite frank I have mixed feelings about Striker because on one level I'm, like, concerned about her spiralling, totally renegade behaviour and stuff, yeah. But on another level, I think she absolutely totally ROCKS.

The rest of the day dragged. I'm boring myself even remembering it. So we all went to Maths and Deathbreath Douglas was scaring us about the GCSEs and how, 'Two years will FLY PAST LIKE A MEEEETEOR!'

Douglas's voice is quite weird and sort of uppy and downy as he's from that Wales place. Y'know, that island near Scotland where they grow those long shallot onion things. I think it belongs to Iceland maybe? Oh, I don't know I'm crap at maps. Douglas pulled me aside at the end and said I would definitely need extra tuition to get a C or above at GCSE and he was sending a letter home to my parents. He recommends two hours per week minimum.

Amazing. Two hours extra each week stuck in a room

with a man with yellow Dracula fangs, a string vest and breath like Satan's bum cleft. THANK YOU DESTINY.

The extra tuition chat happened after French, too. And Biology. And Chemistry. By the time Mr Abdul asked to speak to me 'privately' at the end of Geography I knew what was coming so I said, 'You're out of luck, sorry. I'm already doing twenty hours of private tuition and after-school viola and sculpture too. No more spare life hours left. You're going to have to accept I'll probably fail Geography.'

Mr Abdul snorted loudly at that and said, 'There is NO concept of failure for Hampstead Lycée ladies Miss Montague-Jones, just differing levels of immense success!' Then he said I should look in the post as my parents should be getting a letter. RUDDY WONDERFUL.

The one good thing about today happened when I got home. I opened the front door and an amazing smell wafted up the stairs from the kitchen. Mrs Minsk had made a chicken pie. I ran downstairs and Flash was sitting at the table eating pie with a spoon and Mrs M was filling the dishwasher wearing her dark red, frilly apron that she's worn ever since I was little. Something about that made me feel kind of good.

'Eat!' Mrs M said, pointing at the pie. 'You such a slim thing.'

'I'm so not,' I told her. I think her eyesight is going. She's like sixty or something. Flash asked her the other day if she'd had a pet dinosaur when she was a little girl.

I took a plate and sat down and Mrs M ruffled my hair and said, 'Poppet, I call your mother's assistant, Matthew boy? He very lovely boy, but he say he lost track of your mother three day ago. But he will find her no worry, OK?'

'Cheers, Mrs M,' I sighed. 'I think she might have gone via New York to see Daddy or something. I'm not worried yet.'

'Oh, and your sister Kitten is upstairs, she come home just now,' Mrs M said, sort of shaking her head.

'Yeah, I thought maybe she was,' I said. 'There's, like, a few people hanging about on the steps outside.'

Mrs M just rolled her eyes and so did I, then she ruffled my hair again, and Flash and I sat in the kitchen and finished the pie together.

Flash was drawing a really rather amazing picture of St Paul's Cathedral on his scribble pad with crayons, and I was staring at a pile of Chemistry homework realizing that I didn't understand a single ruddy word of it – NONE OF IT. Something about cracking polymers into ethanol wotsits to produce vegetable oil to make shoes or something. Oh, I don't ruddy know. I'll be bottom of the year again, I know it. Even if mother does buy Mr Abdul tickets to the Wimbledon finals to encourage him to say I'm more like middle of the year. I'll still know the ruddy truth.

'Pop, I have a question,' Flash said to me tonight, adjusting his glasses which had specks of pie gravy on them.

'I'm all ears,' I said. 'Like an elephant. What?'

'Poppet, is it true, right, that if you don't go for a poo for a whole week, then eventually the poo starts to come back up the tunnel and spurt out of your mouth and your ears?'

'Erm, I don't think so Flash,' I said to him.

'Well, where does it go to? What happens to all the poo?' he said.

'I don't know!' I said. 'I think it just comes out of your bum anyway in the end.'

'HOW?' said Flash, looking totally excited. I wish my parents were around to answer this stuff more. I just end up making stuff up.

'I don't know!' I said. 'Maybe the doctor gets it out with a sink plunger!'

Well Flash LOVED this idea and ran off to find his laptop to see if he could see pictures of it happening on YouTube.

Then Mrs M said, 'Poppet, I go watch TV for now and put my feet up. You have friends round tonight or you go out?'

I told her I wasn't sure. Striker is grounded and Vixen is at a fashion show with her big sister Frangipan.

'OK. You need me, you give me a knock,' she said. 'Karina coming back to put Flash to bed.' Then she went into her flat and closed the door. The house was really really quiet. I felt totally completely alone.

I went upstairs to my room. On the third floor,

Kitten's bedroom door was wide open and I could hear the familiar sound of her raspy twenty a day Marlboro Light snoring.

I peeked inside. Kitten was in one of her comas, lying face down on top of her duvet still wearing those high-heeled patent leather boots and last night's tartan mini-dress and neon yellow ripped fishnet stockings which she was wearing in the *Sun* Bizzare column this morning. I tiptoed towards her.

Kitten's skin was sort of porridge coloured and her lips were quite flaky and her blue eye-makeup was all smeared under her eyes. Her right nostril looked sore and it had a bit of blood under it. The blood really freaked me out and it takes a lot to freak me with Kitten these days. Had someone punched her? Was she having a brain haemorrhage?!

I stared at her then picked up her wrist and felt for a pulse and then realized I was being stupid. Kitten had just passed out.

To be totally honest she still looked really really beautiful. Kitten always sort of does. Some newspaper lady last week wrote in *The Times* that my big sister Kitten Calypso Montague-Jones is, 'the most gorgeous girl in London' and that 'every woman wants to be her and every man wants to take her straight to bed'. And that's sort of cool I suppose, isn't it? I just sometimes wish they'd stop quacking on because then she might not get invited to so many parties and do all silly stuff she does because it's starting to get out of control.

I knelt down beside Kitten's bed and picked up a fag that was smouldering away in an ashtray and stubbed it out properly. We didn't need the fire brigade to come again.

'Mumpghghg?' Kitten said, scrunching her face up at me.

I crept in closer and looked at Kit's birthmark on her neck just under her right ear. She usually covers it up with makeup nowadays but I know it's there. Kitten's splodge we call it. When I was a little girl Kitten used to make me press the splodge then she'd go GRRRRRRRROWL like a bear and I'd scream and giggle till I thought I'd nearly choke. It was sort of babyish I guess. We don't do that sort of crap any more.

'Kit, are you awake?' I whispered, sitting down on the bed and moving her hair out of her face.

She snorted a bit and opened one eye.

'Well I am now, aren't I, with all your bloody crashing about! Can't you bugger off and shut the door?'

'Fine,' I said, and then I stomped to my room and got into bed and pulled the duvet round me like I was a tortoise inside its shell and switched my heated underblanket on and decided I was going to sleep RIGHT THEN, which by the way turned out to be IMPOSSIBLE because there were paparazzi mopeds waiting outside the house for Kitten, revving their engines all ruddy night long like a swarm of wasps because apparently – according to TMZ.com – my stupid big sister has been snogging some Hollywood actor called BRANDON GISSAMO who is MARRIED.

So the paparazzi guys were like HONK HONK HONK all night with their horns which was a total BORE, even if it did give me time to write this average day for Dr Sarzberg the therapist, which as I predicted was a waste of time, as all this proves – as I previously said – is that my life is one hundred per cent KILL-YOURSELF-WITH-A-HAMMER-DULL.

There's just no arguing about that is there? I've probably got the most tedious life in the whole ruddy world.

WEDNESDAY 9TH SEPTEMBER

Well, the case of the missing Mummykins has been solved. She's in LIBERIA.

I'd never even heard of the ruddy place before but Flash climbed up a stepladder and pointed it out on the enormous World Map on his nursery wall. Liberia is in Africa. AFRICA? Where Cyril is from!

'Liberia's population is approximately three and half million,' Flash told me today, wiping his runny nose on the cuff of his tiger print sleep suit. 'And the capital is Monrovia.'

'How do you know that?' I said. Flash wrinkled his brow and sighed a bit at me.

'*Everyone* knows that, Poppet,' he said. 'We did capital cities at baby school. Did you not learn them too?'

'Gosh, don't remember,' I said, staring blankly at the map trying to remember anything about kindergarten that didn't involve chasing someone, being chased, screaming or having to leap out of a ballpool jolly quickly as someone had dropped their knickers and done a poo somewhere.

Nope, nothing, not a jot. I feel like this about pretty much all of my time at school.

'So this means that Mother is like, a long way away?' I asked. 'Because when I had her on iCam she said she'd be flying into Heathrow on Friday morning at 11am?'

'She's in Africa, Poppet,' he said.

'About a thousand miles away?' I stared at him, clueless.

'*Three* thousand miles away,' he said, then he wandered off to watch CBeebies. Flash always likes to spend half an hour a morning in his nursery watching CBeebies and drinking chocolate milk and emailing the presenters to correct them on the way they pronounce words. It's sort of sweet I suppose (just not for the blonde girl in rainbow dungarees who's had four emails this month and seems to be off sick right now).

I stood for a while staring at Flash's map and all the different countries. Especially Africa. Africa looks a lot like Kitten's neck splodge. I'm sure Africa was where that Hampstead Lycée girl Imelda Gloringdale (God rest her soul) went on a gap year a few years ago and put her tent up in one of those jungly places and got eaten by a lion. That was, like, totally grim. Apparently you're NOT supposed to wander off into the jungle willy-nilly and start frying sausages, and cooking beans for supper, or so the locals said afterwards when they sent her leftover bits back in a box. Florence, Imelda's sister said it was, like, a really small box. Not a coffin. More like an A4 file you'd buy from Paperchase. Oh Lord. Africa sounds ultra dangerous. What on earth is Mother doing there?

Anyway, it was really cool seeing her face on iCam in her hotel room this morning. The connection was really clear and I could see her tanned skin and blonde hair and her big blue eyes and the white marks her sunglasses had left on her cheeks.

Mother always looks kind of beautiful when she's on holiday. When we were little, Kitten and I used to love looking through mother's travel photos when she got home seeing her looking all happy and glamorous like a different person to how she does when she's dealing with us. I felt weird this morning when I saw her face because suddenly I wanted to say, 'I miss you!' But I didn't as I knew that was just me being whiny and I hate being called the whiny one.

'How are all my babies?' Mother would always ask the nanny on the phone, and the nanny would say, 'Oh they're all doing fine, Mrs Montague, no problems.

45

Poppet is whining a bit, but she'll soon come round, she always does.'

And then Knute and Kitten would say, 'Stop whining, Poppet, you're spoiling Mummy's break. You're always the whiny one.'

I wanted to tell Mother about the blood trickle on Kitten's nose too, but I totally knew she'd tell Kitten I'd told her and then I'd get called a trouble-maker and a grass, so I didn't tell Mother any important things today, I kept it all inside my head where it'll cause least fuss. I just told her about Vixen's Save the Street Cats idea and Mrs M's chicken pie instead. Then I nagged her about the loan for the boob job, but she wasn't going for that one at all.

'No, Poppet,' she said, shaking her head. 'Not yet.'

'Why not?' I said. 'Everyone at the Lycée is having work done!'

OK, this was like, a minor exaggeration, but Livvy in my class had her nose done and tiny cheek implants put in to balance out her face in Year Nine and she looks AWESOME.

'Wait until you're eighteen, give your chest a chance to grow. It might just suddenly sprout,' Mother said as she checked her Blackberry.

Mother is always on her Blackberry sorting out something. She does tonnes of stuff for charities and, like, arranges lunches and stuff, she's always mega-busy.

'Hang on a second, Pop,' she was saying, typing

something and pressing send. 'Oh bloody thing won't send again! Hang on.' Mother was waving the phone above her head and then looking at the screen again. 'Oh it won't go.'

'Email them then,' I said. 'Your laptop is in front of you.'

'My mails aren't coming through on this computer,' said Mother.

'Is that why you haven't replied to mine?' I asked.

Mother rolled her eyes when I said that.

'Sweetie, you haven't sent me any!' she said.

'I so have!' I exclaimed.

'Which account did you send them to? You know I've got three accounts,' she said, looking at the screen again. 'Ooooh! Hooray! It's gone! Sorry what were you saying, Pops?'

'I want a boob job,' I said again.

'As I said, darling, not yet.' Mother smiled as if she'd just had a fabulous idea and added, 'But hey, maybe when you're eighteen we can fly out to California and have some work done together? Just Poppet and Mother, just us two girls! Wouldn't that be fun?'

'Suppose,' I said, trying not to squeal, 'Oh Jesus, please don't YOU have any more work done, Mother. Not on your lips or your brow anyway! You're starting to look so much like Livvy's mummy and Lady Iris's mummy that we all agreed the other day it feels like you're all being played by the same spooky actress or something. No more BOTOX!' But I didn't say that as I knew it would cause a fuss.

'Poppet, shouldn't you be getting ready for school?' Mother asked after a bit.

'No, it's a staff training day today so I'm staying home,' I said.

'Really?' she said. 'OK. Are you doing anything nice?'

I could have so got away with this if I'd wanted, she was looking at the front of her phone again and really distracted, but I'm not a very good liar. I feel too guilty.

'Mother,' I sighed. 'I was just kidding about staff training. I'm going in twenty minutes.'

'Wonderful, darling,' she said. 'Now listen to me, please, Pop. Do please BUCK UP YOUR IDEAS this term. No more letters home banging on about private tuition.'

'Yeah, cool,' I said, cringing.

THREE had arrived already.

'I mean, we know you're not stupid,' she said. 'One can do tests for stupidity at Harley Street and we had those done years ago. You're completely normal! I mean if you had Asperger's or that sort of wotnot it would almost be easier as I could just say, "Look, it's Asperger's", but it's not, is it, Poppet? You're just lazy and you don't listen.'

'Erm, sorry,' I said. 'I drifted off then. What did you say?'

I love that joke. Mother hates it. That's why I do it.

'Very funny,' she said. 'And your English teacher

always says you actually write rather beautifully and you have a strong vocabulary.'

'You gave her a Tiffany teardrop necklace at parents' evening,' I said.

'This was BEFORE THE NECKLACE!' Mother sighed.

She was getting on my nerves now. Of course I've got a bloody good vocabulary I thought. I've grown up in a house full of people who never use one word when twenty-five big words will do.

'And you'll THINK, Poppet,' she said, 'before you pick up a javelin or a crossbow or a hammer or anything that could potentially maim someone this term, won't you, darling?'

'Obviously,' I groaned.

Jesus Christ, you stick one tiny arrow in the cheek of one archery instructor, resulting in an air ambulance and a SMALL AMOUNT OF MICROSURGERY and it haunts you FOR EVER.

'And you'll try to come top of class in lots of subjects won't you and get the Notre Dame Head of House badge?' she said. 'I know you think these things don't matter, Pop, but they really DO.'

'Yeah, cool, no problem,' I said.

'Pearl's daughter Jemima is Head of House at Asquith Ladies and she's done so well out of it. She gets invited everywhere already. She read a psalm from the Bible last Christmas in front of the Queen at Westminster Abbey and attended a lunch afterwards and sat next to Sheikh

Aga Khan of Dubai's son! Her photo was in the social section in *Vogue!*'

'Yeah,' I said. 'Head of House, check. Marry Sheikh Aga Khan's son, check. Yeah, it's all on track,'

'And you'll go to your appointment with Dr Sarzberg and talk to him about things. You'll tell him if you have one of your depressive episodes won't you?' she said.

'I'm not depressed, I'm fine, I just get a bit sad sometimes,' I said. 'It's you who say I've got depression, not me.'

'Good good, darling,' she said taking no notice. 'Look I have to go as I'm having a massage and then I'm having an important meeting. Lots of hugs!'

'Mother, why are you in Liberia?' I said, as she went to close the screen down.

'Oh, Poppet, all will be revealed,' she said, looking all dreamy. 'Let's just say it was a primal urge. A calling!'

'What does that mean?' I said.

'Wait until I get home,' Mother went on. 'We're having a lovely dinner for all of us. I'm getting Matthew to organise it. Email him, won't you? Tell him which restaurant you want to cater it! And Knute is flying home from Climate Camp in Asia tomorrow too! And I've invited Granny. We can all be together! One happy family! Won't that be fun! Oh, darling! Big love to you! Byeeeee!'

Mother waved goodbye and closed the iChat window leaving me more confused than ever before. That's why I went to Flash's nursery to find out where Liberia was. It turns out Liberia is a country that looks like a splodge which is on the other side of the world beside loads of other countries I don't know the names of, or how many people live there, either. I sat for a while and thought about my chances of getting the Notre Dame Head of House badge for academic excellence.

To be quite frank, I've got more chance of flapping my bingo wings and flying to Liberia myself. Seriously.

THURSDAY 10TH SEPTEMBER

I was thinking about Mother's Head of House obsession on my way to hockey today as Vixen, Livvy, Bettina and myself were wandering down the ivy path winding round the back of Godspeed Boys' Academy heading towards the sports block.

I was dragging behind everyone else and Vix kept shouting, 'Pop, hurry up', but I was sort of lost in my head thinking about the Maths lesson we'd just been in, worrying about the equations we'd just been learning, thinking, How can everyone else just DO equations? How does everyone else see a load of random numbers and squiggles on one side of a line and just KNOW that on the other side of the line a different load of numbers and squiggles should be?

And when they've done that how do they always go 'HOT DANG, yes, I get this now! This is amazing, we can use this spangly-equation-stick-it-up-your-bumhole-o-rhythm-wotsit to find how far it is to Jupiter if we went via the moon on rocketboots! Isn't that useful?'

All the while I'm sitting there nodding off into a text book dreaming about something nice for lunch like ravioli. Mmmmmmm ravioli. Mmm nomnomnomnom. I love ravioli.

So Deathbreath Douglas was in a right excitable state today shouting, 'LINEAR SEQUENCES! Once you've got to grips with these little beoooooties, you can conquer the world!'

Then Deathbreath daubed loads of random numbers on the blackboard in a straight line followed by a question mark and shouted, 'What number comes next?' and Lady Iris and the Right Honourable Petronella chucked their hands up and shouted, 'Forty-seven!' and he shouted, 'Very, very good girls!' Then he scribbled some more and said, 'How about this one . . . Vixen?' and Vixen looked up slowly from her Blackberry inside her bag where she was replying to a text from a boy called Rupert she'd met at that Dior Show that her sister was modelling in who's hassling her to meet up for coffee and she batted her long eyelashes at Deathbreath.

'Erm, oh gosh, erm, eighty-two, like, maybe?' she said, which was a complete lucky guess and we all knew it but Douglas smiled anyway.

'Wonderful, Vixen!' and then he wrote another load of numbers down and looked at me and said, 'Poppet, what comes next?' and everyone stared in my direction and I felt my face going nuclear red. No actually, my whole body, starting at my toes and reaching past my belly button which had gone clammy with sweat, then setting fire to my face and the silence was so silent that I could hear an owl in a forest eighty miles away lunching on a fieldmouse.

After what seemed like seven hours of hideous silence I finally said, 'Errrrrrrrrrrrrrm ninety-eight?' Deathbreath looked at me and then looked back at the board as he'd forgotten the answer himself by that point. 'Ninety-eight?' he said, raising an eyebrow.

'Yes, ninety-eight!' I repeated.

'Ninety-eight is the last number in the sequence that I wrote down, Poppet Montague-Jones. WAKE UP!'

And then Livvy coughed and said, 'One-hundred-cough-and-fourty-four cough!' so I shouted 'ONE HUNDRED AND FOURTY-FOUR!' and Mr Douglas tutted at Livvy.

'Thank you, Olivia,' he said, frowning and staring at me. 'I think it's safe to say, Poppet, you won't be out conquering the world any day soon!'

Blitzen and Amelia both laughed like drains at that and Vixen squeezed my knee under the desk and whispered, 'Oh just ignore him, Popsy. Deathbreath hasn't even conquered using a toothbrush.'

What a DISASTER. So I was a bit depressed about all of this today as I was walking along to hockey. The sun was out and it was really quite hot and we all had our blazers off although I had mine folded over my arm and pulled up to my boobs so no one could really get a good look at my ridiculous chest.

Vix on the other hand was in a really good mood today. Vix loves hockey, so she was skipping along wibbling totally random stuff about the sun and how its cosmic rays unite us all and how we should all worship the sun not God or Allah or Buddha (she's bored with being a Buddhist already).

Meanwhile Bettina was messing about doing her zombie walk, where she walks like she's pooed herself dragging one foot behind her shaking her long auburn hair about, and Livvy was extra giddy running ahead and hiding in the longer clumps of ivy growing through the railings then jumping out and doing her fake martial arts moves, the one were she raises both hands up and kicks with one leg shouting, 'Hhhhhhhhhhhaaaaiya' and looks exactly like an epileptic tree.

Then Livvy did that thing she does where she pretends the ivy is attacking her, pulling her in, and she shouts, 'GET YOUR BRANCHES OFF MY HAIRYMARY YOU DIRTY PIG!' She's been doing that since Year Seven and it never gets any less funny.

Girls at Hampstead Lycée always say that the girls on the Snotingham Estate reckon all of us at the Lycée are a bunch of snobs and we just walk about with our noses in the air going, 'Fwah fwah fwah my papa owns the Isle of

Wight', and we never even have a laugh at break times as we're so up ourselves and this is really unfair and not true at all. Sometimes I really wish the Snotingham girls could see stuff like Livvy fighting with an ivy bush shouting, 'IT'S BLOODY GOT ME AGAIN, POP!' then turning up to class fifteen minutes late with leaves in her knickers and sticking out of her hair and telling the teacher she's been sexually molested by a bush and will be giving birth to a bonsai tree in nine months time. I don't think we're that sensible at all to be honest. I think a lot of the time we're actually total ruddy loons.

So, as I'm walking along the ivy path today I spot that Vixen and the girls up ahead have come to a halt and are peering through the ivy and lots of other Lycée girls are swarming about squeaking and screaming too. Well this could only mean one thing: the boys from Godspeed Academy are between lessons and out on the school grounds roaming wild.

Ggngngn, I thought to myself. I was having a testing time enough today without the Godspeed knobheads lurking about being their usual pain in the butt selves. And they are COMPLETE AND UTTER PAINS IN THE BUTT.

At least, I definitely still think they are and always will be. But by the end of Year Nine, Striker, Vixen, Livvy and Bettina had started chatting with some of the more human ones. Boys like Jackdaw, Hal and Max who are now in Year Eleven.

They've even started being almost friends with some of them, which seems ruddy ironic to me when we've spent the past three years running terrified down that ivy path trying to avoid being poked with sticks and spat on. Not forgetting of course the BRUTAL Baked Potato Incident, in which a potato thwacked me on the forehead ALMOST PUTTING ME IN A COMA. Marmaduke Adams will pay for that. Oh yes, believe me, he will. He is on my list of REVENGE. I just haven't worked out how or when yet. It may involve simply transporting a larger, more intimidating vegetable, say a pumpkin or maybe a prize-winning marrow, to his house and firing it out of a cannon at him and blasting his smug head clean off. I believe a small amount of time spent in Holloway Women's Prison for murdering Marmaduke is probably worth it.

I'd be totally happy in Holloway anyway as there's no boys and you get to lie on a bunk bed all day snoozing for months on end and you can grow your armpit hair long and be fat and have no boobs if you want, and no one expects you to chisel a Roman Centaur out of a block of ruddy marble in an after-school sculpture class. Prison sounds rather better than my life now. One hundred per cent FACT.

So anyway, back to the Godspeed Academy boys. I basically struggle to see the point of them – aside from Felix Hayes-Burlington who's a good friend but he's different. The rest of them, MEH. Because if they're not being horrid, smelly pigs and making you feel rubbish, they're being all nice smelling and hot and charming but totally up themselves like Jackdaw Penry from Year Eleven who was standing right up at the ivy railings today, being all, 'Hey, I'm Jackdaw, feast on my male pheromones', making all the Hampstead Lycée girls lose the ability to breathe and speak properly just by existing on earth.

Lady Iris, bless her, seemed frozen in time, with her mouth open drowning gnats in drool from the moment he appeared.

Vixen never behaves like that. Even though Jackdaw was standing right by her being all tall and dark haired and wide-shouldered, fixing his enormous brown eyes right on her, quacking on about a party that he wanted her to go to at the end of the month that his brothers are throwing in Chelsea at their father's nightclub, Voyage. Well Vixen's face didn't look even slightly flushed. Vixen never blushes. Her skin is always honey brown. This is an amazing skill. Me, I can start blushing when I'm all by myself just REMEMBERING a situation where I blushed. In fact at the Year Ten End-of-Year Mixer between Hampstead Lycée and Godspeed Academy this boy called Crispin snuck his arm around my shoulder when we were all chatting in the cloakrooms and he played with my neck with his finger and my whole face went so VIOLET that he looked at me and said, 'Oh my God, I think you're having an allergic reaction to something!' Then he dumped me back with Striker (who was behind a cooker in Godspeed school kitchens with some random Godspod having more than her neck tickled) and he RAN AWAY. My face looks like a jar of beetroot just writing this.

Anyway, it turns out that Jackdaw Penry's party was to celebrate the Penry family's hot new business venture (something about yachts? Building yachts? Racing Yachts? Putting furniture in yachts? Can't remember now). Jackdaw was saying that Vixen should come along and bring all her girlfriends as, 'We need beautiful ladies on the red carpet so we get into all the newspapers.'

Then Jackdaw took a business card out of his blazer pocket and passed it through the ivy. Vixy just smiled and said sort of distractedly, 'Oh bless you, Jackdaw, cheers, I'll check with my girls. We're probably booked up that night though.' This was a total lie but it made us sound really mature and in demand. In reality, Livvy's tongue was out almost drooling on to the flagstone path, Striker was grounded, and the only thing in my diary was extra equations with Deathbreath and going to Harley Street to have raspberry jam pips hoovered out of my brace.

'Call me, I'll put you on the VVVIP list,' Jackdaw said. 'I'll get you a table and bottle of Cristal.'

Our own table? That bit sounded sort of good actually, but I wasn't letting him see that so I just shrugged as though I didn't care either way.

'Thanks, Jackdaw,' Vixen said, tossing the card in her

school bag then checking her phone as if she'd forgotten about his boring party already. Vix is so good at this type of thing. No boy ever really knows what's going on inside Vixy's head.

Just then something horrible happened. Marmaduke Adams appeared at the fence. I was sort of shocked when I saw him as he seemed to be a lot taller than last year, like he'd suddenly shot up to being man-size overnight. Marmaduke had turned up the collar on his shirt and his navy blazer and his tie was pulled tight, sort of skinny, and he'd let his brown hair grow very long. In fact, afterwards some of the girls were saying Marmaduke was looking sort of hot. MARMADUKE ADAMS? HOT!!? This is the boy who once in Year Seven found a dog turd and brought it to school in a plastic box and got onto the ivy path on the Hampstead Lycée side and stuck matches into it and set it alight just as the break bell went, so some poor girl stamped it out and didn't see that poo was all over her shoes.

Marmaduke is a nutjob. And now girls are saying he's dreamy?

'Wat' up, bitches,' he said as he wandered up. We all just groaned at him.

'Look, you've got to come to Jackdaw's night. Gran Patron Tequila are sponsoring so there's going to be gallons of free cocktails. I'm going to get you all slaughtered and then sex-pest you all up one by one.' Maramduke put out his hands and mimed groping a big pair of boobs while pulling his best pervert face, which in fairness isn't much different from his normal face as Marmaduke just looks like a grade A pervert FULL STOP. Livvy squealed with laughter when he said that, like she actually wouldn't mind being sex-pested at all.

'No seriously ladies,' he said, eyeing up Livvy. 'Every party needs some hotties on the guest list.' Then he stopped and pretended he'd just noticed me standing there and said, 'Oh sorry, Poppet, didn't see you standing there! Don't worry, there's always room for one goat in a dress.'

Well my face started to feel hot immediately.

'Whatever, Marmapuke,' I said to him, then I turned my face and started to walk away.

'Oh, Marmaduke? What the hell? You really are a knob,' sighed Vixen. 'Come on girls we're going.'

'Oh bloody relax, Vixen, it was a joke,' said Marmaduke.

We all started walking but Marmaduke was laughing really loudly, and Jackdaw was kicking his ankle to try and keep him quiet but no one keeps Marmaduke quiet and he's so damn FUNNY all the funniness has to come flowing out like a big hilarity tsunami.

'Hey, Poppet, ask your big sister Kitten if she's free, will you?' Marmaduke shouted after me.

I could hear other boys whistling and laughing when he said that and Jackdaw saying, 'Oh shut it, Marmo', but Marmaduke just carried on.

'Hey, I see Kitten's given up wearing her knickers lately. I saw that photo of her falling out of a Merc in the *Sun* last week. The one where you could see her beaver! HAHAHAHAHAH! You should dress more like that. I'd like that a lot!'

My face was purple now. People don't really mention my sister to me much at school. Kitten is a personal no go area. I mean, yeah, fine, everyone knows who Kitten is. She's in the papers every day. But I don't like talking about her, well apart from to Vixen and Striker, but not really to anyone else, as Kitten does some pretty ridiculous things and I don't even bloody understand them so how can I explain it to anyone else? Like the time during summer when Kitten got barbed-wire tattooed round the top of her thigh with, 'LOVE FENCE' written at the top right near her Mary. What was that about? She said it was the title of a song some boy had written about her, and she doesn't even speak to him now. Then there was the time just after last Christmas when she slapped a bartender in Claridges hotel for refusing to serve her a Martini as she was drunk already and Daddy had to go and collect her from West End Central police station! That was just completely embarrassing.

Since Kitten's had access to her trust fund she's spent, like, hundreds and hundreds of thousands of pounds of it but she can't even explain where! She just says it's on her 'lifestyle' and I'm a nosy brat and I'll understand one day when I ever go anywhere more exciting than my room. I've repeated some of this to Mother and Father but they just say that Kitten is being young and going through a wild stage and they went through crazy stages too so we have to give Kitten 'space' to do it and try not to get angry with her. And I sort of get that I suppose. But it doesn't mean the stuff Marmaduke says makes me feel any less like throwing-up.

'Poppet, it was a joke,' Marmaduke shouted, then he rattled the fence a bit wanting me to look at him, but I wasn't in the mood.

'Go and die somewhere,' Bettina shouted, dragging me along as we all walked away with our noses in the air.

'He's such a retard,' said Vix.

'Yeah,' Livvy said, turning behind to get one last look at him.

'Look, don't you worry, Pop. Karma is so going to strike that boy down,' Vix said, putting her arm round my shoulder as we walked off. 'It's going to hit him like a herd of trampling wildebeest. I can't wait.' This didn't sounds very Buddhist but it made me feel a little bit better.

Later on in the changing room we all examined the card Jackdaw had given to Vix, and Livvy was saying that we should definitely go to Jackdaw's party as it sounded like fun and then Vixen was saying, 'Actually, Mummy is bound to let me go if it's Jackdaw, she LOVES Jackdaw's father. They've been friends since like back in the day.' Then Bettina texted Striker to see if she'd be off her grounding by October and Striker texted back 'YES!!! And if I'm not. I'll just sneak out the fourth floor window and slide down the drainpipe. Done it before was EZEE-PEEZY-BOTTY-SQUEEZY.' Everyone was being giddy again cooing about how mature Jackdaw is to have a business card and passing it round the whole changing room and staring at the title which said 'Jackdaw Penry – Impresario', which Bettina reckoned made him sound totally HOT like an ultra important international business man.

I just tutted and said it didn't, it just made Jackdaw sound like a totally gay cruise-ship magician.

SATURDAY 12TH SEPTEMBER

My mother is home from Liberia. She was in the kitchen today when I got home from the Lycée yesterday, looking all pink-nosed and jetlagged and bordering on insane wearing an emerald green African kaftan thingy she'd had made especially for her by Liberian locals. Mother seemed to think the kaftan made her look exactly like The Queen of Liberia, but Flash and I agreed later on that it made her look like an enormous pickled gherkin.

Luckily Mummy had had me an identical one made too, so now we can float about Hampstead High Street together looking like clouds of green toxic gas and people can say, 'Oh look at Jocasta Montague-Jones and her daughter, aren't they alike? Those kaftans are exactly the same! Wow, they're like sisters!' (This will never happen. NEVER. I am giving mine to Mrs Minsk to make into rags to polish the toilet with.)

'My beautifullll bay-biieeeees,' Mother kept bleating when we got home, then she grabbed Flash and I by the necks and pulled us into an extreme Mummy-hug and my face got lost in the middle of her bosom which was really rather scary as the ridge on the saline bag inside her left boob was blocking my nostrils and I almost started to suffocate.

'Have you been having LOTS of fun, Poppet?' she kept saying, which is what Mother always says when she gets back from somewhere far away, kind of missing the point that it's *her* who has been away on the razzle having fun and me that's been here for three weeks living on lemon curd sandwiches, sleeping with a bipolar labrador and getting my fingers chopped up with a hockey stick for having the brazen cheek to try to stop Blitzen Trapper scoring a goal. Not that I'm slagging Blitzen if she ever reads this, she totally didn't mean it. It was an accident. I'm pretty sure.

'What happened to your fingers?' Mother said, grabbing my right hand which Matron had bandaged up for me as there was a load of skin all ripped off and it looked utterly YAK.

'Oh, nothing,' I said to Mother. 'Blitzen smacked me on the knuckles with a stick. She didn't mean it.'

'Blitzen Trapper?' Mother asked, walking off to get a bottle of gently carbonated Badoit water from our enormous pink Smeg fridge. 'I saw her father in the Virgin club class lounge at Heathrow on my way out. He's terribly charming isn't he? What do his company make again?'

'Something to do with guns,' I said. 'He makes guns and sells them to people or something.'

'He MANUFACTURES guns and sells them to various countries,' Flash chipped in. Flash knows all kinds of random stuff like this. 'He owns Trapper Aerospace Inc.'

'How do you know that?' I said.

'Everybody knows that, Poppet,' tutted Flash, adjusting his glasses. 'It's on Wikipedia. Although I do accept the sources on that site need to be verified inde-pen-dently.'

Mother and I stared at Flash. There was a silence. Flash opened a bag of Cadbury's Chocolate Buttons and pushed three into his tiny mouth.

'Well, they've got an adorable house in Fort Lauderdale in Florida. He showed me a photo,' said Mother, getting her Blackberry out of her enormous Louis Vuitton carry-on bag. 'He's American, isn't he? His accent is hard to place.'

'Yeah,' I said, wishing I'd not let Mother grope my hand as it felt like it was bleeding again. 'But Blitzen's mother is Russian.'

'Oh . . . right, I see that now.' My Mother said smiling. 'You can tell there's Russian blood in there, can't you? Such amazing poise Blitzen has, hasn't she? She can really walk. I've seen her walking into the school gates. She's like a catwalk model.'

I felt a bit annoyed when she said that. I'm not sure why. Just the way her face lit up at the thought of Blitzen walking. My mother's phone was ringing now and she was trying her best to ignore it but she couldn't.

'Oh I can walk too,' I said. 'Walking is easy. Look I'm doing it now.'

I took a few steps to show her. Then I clomped past the Aga and back again. 'Look Mother, I'm walking!'

'Oh, don't be so wilfully fractious, Poppet, you know what I mean. Blitzen can walk like a runway model,' Mother said, before picking up her phone and answering it with a loud, 'JOCASTA MONTAGUE-JONES!' Then, 'Yes, what?! You've sourced the tiles for the dairy parlour? Oh you are an angel! Yes, I'm flying out to Tuscany in ten days to project manage it!' She waved her hand at me to shut-up but I carried on talking anyway.

'Walking is one thing I'm probably good at,' I said, 'I just put one foot after the other, clomp, clomp clomp.' Mother just wrinkled her nose and moved to the far end of the kitchen. 'And I try not to let my face get too close to the ground as that would be called, well, falling over.'

'Sebastian,' my mother sighed, 'I'm going to have to

call you back. It's terribly noisy here. Yes, I'm back in London now. Yes, surrounded by kids. I know.' Then she stomped up to her office and the door slammed.

Mother left at the right time because just then Octavia Square got even noisier still. The front door swung open and Macbeth suddenly went BONKERS barking and howling and screeching like a pig, then Mrs M shouted, 'Is Knute! Knute is home! He home from Climate Camp. Oh my God I go run bath he is feelthy like a gorilla!'

And then Knute tumbled in through the front door shouting, 'HELLO FAMILY' and suddenly the house was EXTRA LOUD again after weeks of it being like a big empty echoey place that even a ghost wouldn't bother to haunt as it would develop clinical depression.

Knute dropped his enormous rucksack and turned to shut the front door and a paparazzi guy who was being ruddy cheeky, coming almost right INSIDE THE RUDDY HOUSE when they KNOW they're not meant to do that and we got a bloody legal injunction against them at one point, was shouting, 'Knute, just one more please? Knute, could you turn and pick up the rucksack again, please, oh go on, please, it'll make my editor happy.'

Knute, as ever, was really lovely and did as he was asked and made a peace sign like he always does in paparazzi shots despite the fact I've told him a thousand times it makes him look at least forty years old and not very cool at all. Knute always laughs uproariously when I say that. 'I'm here to save the planet, Popsicle,' he says, 'not be cool.'

Eventually Knute got the door shut and Macbeth was off the hook with happiness by now running up and down the living-room, then up and down the stairs into the kitchen trying to lick Knute's face and plonk her big paws on his shoulders, basically making it plain that two weeks trapped with me has been a collosal DRAG and all my 5am expeditions to the back garden stood in my pyjamas under an umbrella trying to persuade the stupid thing to pee and poo were basically forgotten as HER LORD AND MASTER WAS HOME!

Knute was saying, 'Have you been a good girl for Aunty Poppet, Macbeth? HAVE YOU? HAVE YOU!' and Macbeth was barking as if to say 'YES!' and Knute was saying, 'OhBethywethywethywoooo!' and Macbeth was rolling over on her back and waving her paws in the air and letting out yelps and Knute was tickling her belly and make her ears into a pile of fur on her head and then blowing raspberry noises into the fur and Macbeth was wild with happiness and in the end I told Knute that him and Macbeth should get a ruddy room and snog as they were so deeply in love. Knute snorted a bit. 'Oh do you want a cuddle too, Popsicle?!' he said, and he grabbed me and kissed me on the forehead and I laughed and screamed at him to get off as he smelled of bonfires and cheesy feet and sweat.

Knute looked ruddy exhausted. Knute says he's been

banging a drum and honking a kazoo outside an important politician's home in Tutong in Brunei, south-east Asia for the last two weeks to persuade the man to make the Sultan of Brunei think seriously about energy-friendly lightbulbs.

So I said to Knute, 'The Sultan can't use those lightbulbs, can he? What if someone started to attack the palace in the middle of the night? It'd take forty minutes for the lights to come on properly, he'd not be able to find his slippers let alone load an Uzi.'

'You obviously know very little about the new types of energy-efficient lightbulbs, Poppet,' said Knute, and I thought to myself, Well I know that me and Mrs M took them all out when you went away and swapped them for sixty watt ones. And we've been tearing round the house with stepladders putting them back since we heard your flight landed. I didn't say that though as the truth often causes a fuss in this place.

So then Knute asked me what I'd been doing and I tutted loudly and said, 'I've just been at after-school Geography class looking at a picture of an oxbow lake for a whole hour which is basically a puddle on a mountain with no use at all except for crows to drink from. IT WAS CRAP. In fact at some points during that lesson I felt like hanging myself with my Lycée tie.'

Knute sniggered and said, 'Well you're a little ray of sunshine as ever! Would your present cheer you up?'

I totally perked up then and said, 'ALWAYS!' and

Knute opened his case and took out two bags and passed one of them to me. It was bulky but really light. I pulled at the cellotape and opened it up to find . . . a TEDDY BEAR. I got it out of the bag and stared at it, then turned it around a few times just to check it wasn't a teddy bear with a bottle of rum inside it that I could slurp on my own just to brighten up *EastEnders*. But no it was a plain old teddy bear made by a local South-east Asian person who'd jammed one eye on a bit wonky and sewn the mouth on crooked so it had a slightly perverted expression. It looked a bit like Maramduke Adams in teddy bear form. Not that Marmaduke will be reincarnated as a teddy bear. He'll be reincarnated as a swamp-dwelling warthog that eats old rotting fruit and used sanitary pads.

I looked at the bear and did my best not-disappointed face.

'Do you like him?' said Knute, pointing at the bear.

'I love him, Knute, thank you,' I fibbed, and then I gave my big brother a hug. Sand fell out of Knute's jumper when he bent down to cuddle me. I stared at the teddy again and it pulled a face which seemed to say, 'If I give you all the answers to the SAT tests can I put my hand up near your hairymary?'

'I knew you'd like him,' Knute said. 'You love bears don't you?'

'Yeah,' I said, 'I always did.'

I love my big brother Knute an awful lot but

sometimes I feel he's missing the fact that I'm like, not little any more. In fact last month when Knute's friend Roddy met me at the Octavia Square summer barbecue he asked Knute how old I was and Knute thought for a while then said, 'You're about ten or eleven aren't you, Pop?'

TEN OR ELEVEN! I was mortified! I put a rolled up tennis sock in my bra for a week after that and started wearing high-heels around the house which didn't make me look much older, but totally aggravated my ingrown toenail.

'So this Climate Camp thingy?' I said to Knute. 'Did you, like, win this one then or whatever?'

'Oh yeah! Epic win for us! Mr Underpant-a-gogo (OK, this is what it sounded like Knute called him) was driven MENTAL by our clanging and banging and he agreed to fall in line with the Kyoto Agreement on climate change, so yeah . . . we won this one, Pops! WE RULE!' Knute said this was maybe one of the proudest moments of his entire life.

'Even more proud than when you handcuffed yourself to Sir Hugh who ran that GlobalNation Chemical Inc. place and it was in all the papers?'

Knute thought for a bit and said, 'OK, the same amount of proud as that, that was bloody completely hilarious.' And then we both giggled lots although it wasn't at all funny at the time as Daddy was supposed to be playing golf with Sir Hugh that Sunday and he had to cancel as Knute had swallowed the key to the handcuffs and they were both at the police station waiting for it to come out in Knute's poo, which was extra embarrassing as Knute couldn't even have the poo without the international president of GlobalNation Chemical Inc. standing in the toilet cublicle with him with his remaining free hand over his nose.

That was when loads of my friends started to really fancy Knute, 'cos he was even on the cover of the *Style* magazine in the *Sunday Times* and they called him 'Britain's Hottest Eco-Warrior' and had a photo of him with nothing on except metallic green body paint and his hands in golden handcuffs.

This was over a year ago, but I found a copy of it underneath Striker's bed last week and it was all crumpled and grubby like she's been kissing it or GOD KNOWS what else every night, as the magazine was VERY 'well thumbed'.

So, last night we had the, ahem, 'lovely dinner' that Mother had asked Matthew, her assistant, to plan. Matthew had done an amazing job considering how vague Mother can be with instructions. He'd left tonnes of messages with Kitten and he'd managed to lure Granny over from Belgravia and he'd even made the catering people lay an extra place for Daddy and set a MacBook open at Daddy's usual place and dialled him in on iChat so we could see him on iCamera eating an enormous salt beef bagel and drinking coffee while we all yaddered around him and picked at the olives and houmous and flat breads starter.

I was sitting beside Daddy and he was asking me about school so I told him the truth that I feel like the class idiot and I hate the place and he laughed at me, just like Knute did, as if it must be me having a joke.

Daddy's beard has grown quite long and fuzzy since I last saw him. He looks a lot like a caveman but with thick black glasses. Like a caveman who works in a laboratory maybe. Daddy was checking another iChat screen as we were talking and saying things to his assistant Georgina who I've never met as she only works with him in the Spike Media Global Network offices in New York, even though she is British. I think she lives there now. She kept coming over to give him things and he kept making jokes with her and at one point she leaned in to give him a piece of paper and I heard her say, 'Please don't put me on camera, this is far too heavy.'

I wondered what she meant by that, but then I thought maybe Daddy has probably told her about our family dinners and how they always get heavy, which they always ALWAYS do.

And bless Matthew as he really really tried to make this dinner all light and happy but he doesn't seem to grasp that my family is totally incapable of being all light and happy long-term, and we never all sit in the same room together for a long time without at least one person getting all stress-heady and going, 'Ooh boo hoo me! No one cares about my feelings BOO-HOO-HOO!' (They don't actually say BOO-HOO they say lots of other words but what it sounds like after you've sat through a few of these sessions is just a lot of boo-hooing.)

So then someone else slaps the table and says, 'Boo-hoo you? Boo-hoo your feelings? Well what about boo-hoo me! My feelings are much more BOO-HOO-HOO!'

Then after a tremendous amount of BOO-HOO has been booed and hooed someone always has to storm out of the room as their boo-hooing has became so enormous and serious it can't be contained to one room and it simply must be spread around the house via the process of slamming doors and crying. (This is usually either Mother or Kitten, though other people, like Knute or myself or Granny, are prone to joining in now and then.)

I feel sorry for Dr Sarzberg to be honest, as his job is to listen to all of my family's boo-hooing and then try to make it all better, which he's making a massive pig's ear of at the moment because after last night's disaster things are clearly getting worse.

So, we're all eating and chatting and Granny is at the end of the table drinking a large gin and tonic in a high ball glass with ice and cucumber and cackling about what she said to these people from the Tate Modern art gallery this morning when they called up asking to loan one of her Picassos for an exhibition next January. The Tate heard she's got a few Picassos in her private collection and were wondering if she would consider showing them to the public in a show next year. Well actually, someone had tipped them off that she keeps one of the Picassos in a downstairs toilet and they were gently suggesting it might be better looked after by them, than next to a loo being splashed by wee and steeped in bum fumes.

'So, what did you say?' I said to Granny.

'Well, I told them to BLADDY GO AWAY of course, sweetie!' Granny cackled, speaking in that amazing way Granny does which is how rich people do in films but not usually in real life, as in real life rich people don't sound so crazy posh, in fact most girls at my school try to make their voices a bit more, well, street, and some girls even say 'innit' (although it sounds a bit weird). One girl Tabitha started saying, 'Aks' instead of 'Ask' in a Caribbean way, until her parents got a letter home from the Parent Teacher governing board and she got sent to Knightsbridge for elecution lessons.

I suppose what I'm trying to say is that most of us don't want to sound all grand and up-ourselves like privileged little princesses, but Granny is totally old-school and she's completely who she is. She sounds exactly like the Queen. Or, well, how the Queen would speak if she drank about half a bottle of Hendricks gin every lunchtime and then called up the Tate Modern to swear at them just for her own amusement.

Granny doesn't really act like the Queen either (or

Lizzie as Granny calls her), because the Queen does all sorts of those important Commonwealth visit thingies, when she flies for fifteen hours and gets out of an aeroplane in a big hat and says, 'HELLOOOO! I AM THE QUEEN, PLEASE SHOW ME SOME BUILDINGS AS I REALLY MUST SEE THEM AND SHAKE HANDS WITH EVERYONE PLEASE!'

No, Granny doesn't do any of these visits because she's only Lady Octavia Montague, which is eighty-fourth in line to the throne, and that involves doing nothing really apart from an awful lot of cocktail parties and horse-racing events and lying about in her huge mansion in Belgravia all day, sometimes wearing a tiara for no reason at all, pondering which bottle of vintage Chateau Neuf Du Pape that her butler Guillame should bring her up from her cellar for dinner.

Granny's life is quite bizarre really. She doesn't do any real work like Mummy does. Like, throw parties for charity or anything. That's why Mummy says I should try to become brilliant at sculpting or the viola or something so I have a purpose in life and not end up like Granny.

'Granny,' I said into her ear as she's almost seventy-three now and is occasionally hard of hearing, though it's hard to remember this sometimes as she always wears an amazing black wig set into curls and big diamond earrings so she looks a lot younger. 'You ARE going to lend the Tate people that Picasso aren't you? You're so naughty.'

Granny did her cackle again, and said, 'Oh of course I am, Poppet. I was just teasing. They can take it tomorrow. Damned hideous thing. The insurance people keep nagging me to take it out of the toilet in the east wing or at least put extra alarms in, but I've told them that the bladdy burglars can have it! I said to Pablo when he gave it to me, I said, "Darling don't give it to me, I'm a philistine with art, I'll not appreciate it", but he did anyway. And just look at it! It's supposed to be me holding a cat! I've got two bloody noses and six breasts! But Pablo was a dear old fool and he was awfully soft about me so I shouldn't be mean.'

'You *knew* Pablo Picasso?' I said.

'Yes, of course, the girls, Frances and Tilly and I, were in Paris an awful lot in the 1950s. Frances had an apartment literally overlooking the Champs Elysee. We had such fun.' Granny signalled for the waiter to bring her some champagne. 'Pablo was always around. We went to the same parties.'

I sat for a bit thinking about this. My art teacher is obsessed with Picasso. I wondered whether taking the painting into the Lycée as a 'show and tell' might make my grades any higher. Like that lifetime membership to the Tate Modern Private Members Bar helped get me a B last year.

'Anyway, let's have a glass of Bollinger,' said Granny. 'It'll take the edge off this bladdy dreadful family dinner.'

'Poppet shouldn't be drinking! She is FIFTEEN,' my

father shouted through the computer speakers. I'd forgotten he was listening.

'Oh, nonsense James, she's having a glass of champagne with her grandmother,' Granny tutted to the laptop. 'What's dinner without a lovely drink? A wholly redundant experience, that's what! Poppet, how do I turn this thing off?'

'Mother, don't shut that laptop,' my mother shouted. 'You promised you'd behave yourself.'

Daddy just rolled his eyes and started checking his other screen again. Then the catering staff started serving the food, which was from Mummy's favourite vegan place, that she's totally in love with, called Chosen Leaf in Chelsea. The main course was quinoa with baby artichokes, almonds and cranberries and all sorts of other beans and curd and herb dishes that makes you fart like a racehorse immediately after you've swallowed them.

This wasn't my choice at all. I definitely told Matthew I wanted Thai green curry and pad thai and sticky rice from Busaba Ethai in Soho, but my choice must have been vetoed as ever. I don't know why I bother even speaking sometimes. But, the fact is that everyone was getting along and we were all eating and chatting and Flash was making us all laugh telling us about some spelling bee that he's in at school and how he's been asked to sit it out to give the other children a chance and suddenly Mummy said, 'Oh, Flash, you really are the brains of the family! I'm so proud of you. In fact, I'm incredibly proud of all my babies! Just look at you! I've got a future NASA rocket scientist here and he's only six years old! And I've got a famous eco-warrior! And Kitten is a globally famous society It girl! And I've got Poppet who ... erm ...' Then Mother looked at me for a moment and came to a halt and picked up her wine glass to stall for time and there was a terribly awkward silence until, thankfully, Granny jumped in and said in her amazingly loud drunk way, 'We have Poppet Zanzibar Montague-Jones who is an individual, a thinker and is blessed with a heart as big as England. Not many of *those* around these parts I can tell you. Three cheers for Poppet Zanzibar I say! Hip hip hooray!'

Granny waved her glass in the air and Mummy looked round at the serving staff and swiped her hand across her throat and mouthed, 'NO MORE CHAMPAGNE FOR THAT ONE.'

Finally, Mummy clinked her glass and stood up and said she needed to say a few important words to us all about recent events. Then she started waffling on about how the last few weeks of her life had been, 'her most crucial quest of personal discovery' and how she was never even supposed to go to Liberia in Africa, she was only supposed to be going to Antigua in the Caribbean to gather her thoughts for her new interior design project. HOWEVER, when she was in Antigua there were a few very rainy days and there was no chance of going to the beach and the spa treatments were all booked up, which meant she had to just lie in her suite and read magazines all day long. Well one of the magazines she'd taken from the hotel lobby was an old copy of the magazine *National Geographic*. And there was an incredibly 'moving' feature about the African country Liberia and the terrible poverty and horrors that have happened since the civil war. And she read about the thousands of babies and children in orphanages lying on wee-drenched mattresses, covered in scabies, with rumbling stomachs, as their parents had simply dumped them as they couldn't look after them. Or they'd died of AIDS or Malaria.

Well Granny pushed away her quinoa at this point and said to Mother, 'Dear God, Jocasta, lighten up, sweetie, will you? This food is revolting enough without you grizzling on about bedbugs.'

Mummy tutted and said to Granny, 'Mother don't be deliberately obtuse! What have we agreed about you mocking my thoughts and inspirations? Dr Sarzburg talked to you about that when we had that mother/daughter session, didn't he?'

Granny laughed like a seagull and said, 'Oh bladdy Dr Sarzberg! I'm not taking orders off a bladdy German. We all know where that leads to. That's the mistake the Poles made in 1939.'

Then Knute piped up with, 'Hey Granny, the Germans are actually like really, really lovely people. It's the

Germans we should be taking notice of. They've actually learned a lot from their history.'

At this point Mother started getting cross and saying she hadn't finished her very important life-changing story, but she didn't get any further as suddenly the door to the dining-room fell open and bundle of something sort of fell in.

IT WAS KITTEN.

Kitten, I think it's safe to say, was not expecting to see us. It was almost like she'd just leaned against the door and fallen into the room accidentally. She was wearing a dark red ballet tutu, black footless tights, a black fur hat and yellow plastic Jesus sandles. I recognized the outfit from that evening's *London Lite* gossip page. They'd printed a photo of her getting money out of a cashpoint in Soho earlier that day, with stockist details of where to buy every single item she had on and a little article saying how Kitten Calypso Montague-Jones is, 'one of the world's most desirable names to have on your party guest list, especially since Kitten's recent alleged affair with married actor Brandon Gissamo which she vehemently denies'. Anyway, by last night, Kitten's face was sort of grubby, and her eyes had black rings under them. She looked ill.

'Mummy!' Kitten said, looking completely confused, then trying to walk forwards, but actually falling across the room, before trying to turn around and escape back out of the door again.

This is when we realized she wasn't alone. There was someone lurking in the hallway.

'Kitten, come in and get some dinner!' Mother said. 'Bring your friend! Who's out there with you?'

'It's Steel. We were just coming to, er, pick up something,' Kitten said. Her eyes were as big as dinner plates.

'Steel, come in and say hello then, darling,' said Mother.

Steel shuffled into the room. I recognized him from the gossip columns too. He was about six feet tall and he has longish black hair which was crimped and backcombed and was either greasy or covered in oil. He was wearing a blue fur coat and shoes with long pointy toes and his skin was sort of grey. I'm sure he's in a band and he was on the cover of the *Dazed and Confused* magazine I once stole from Kitten's room to read on the loo.

Steel looked sort of terrified when he saw us, then he sniffed loudly and got a pile of tissues out of his pocket.

'Hello, Steel!' Mother barked. 'Do sit down and join us for some dinner please!'

'Mnpghgh, OK, cheers,' said Steel, who was grinding his teeth and sucking in his cheeks like he'd had too much coffee.

'Steel?' said Mummy, suddenly having a brain wave. 'You're not Zane Drum's son by any chance? Zane who played with Yellow Dawn in the 1980s?'

Steel nodded, going bright red. 'Yeah that's him pghghsplgh badumsh,' he muttered.

'Oh heavens! I remember you when you were a baby! You're the same age as Knute. Your mother and I used to take you both to the same birthday parties at the Groucho Club in the West End. You were always getting lost under the bar or escaping out of the building! We once found you wandering down Old Compton Street on your own! You were a real scamp.'

Steel didn't say anything to that, he just nodded and sweated like he was having a very, very bad experience indeed. A bit like when you have a nightmare where you're in the road naked with your butt on show for all to see.

'How is your mother?' Mummy asked. 'Is she still interior designing?'

'Shumph in Cornwall,' Steel mumbled. 'She mumph organic candles. Keeps bees and mumpghy schlump does reiki healing and stuff mumpgh.'

'Fabulous,' said my mother. 'Sit down both of you!'

Kitten and Steel looked at each other in horror then stumbled towards the table and slouched down on seats.

Kitten suddenly looked to her left and right and jumped a little in fright. 'Wow, Granny, what the hell?' she said. Then she looked around at all of us and said, 'Flash, Knute, Poppet? Is that Daddy on the laptop? What's going on? Did someone die?'

'We're having a special family dinner, Kitten!' said

Mother. 'Didn't you get Matthew's message?'

'He didn't send *me* any messages,' Kitten grumped.

'Yes he did, darling,' said Mother. But Kitten just tutted and said, 'I've got about eight different email addresses, Mother, because they keep getting hacked into by journalists.' At this point the waiter put plates of food down in front of Steel and Kitten, which they both stared at as though they were looking at a plate of maggots stewed with bum-boils.

Steel tried to show willing by picking up a fork and chasing some round a plate unenthusiastically. He took a tiny mouthful and chewed like he was trying not to let his tastebuds come into contact with it.

'Anyway!' said Mother. 'Where was I? Yes, LIBERIA. So I was reading this article about the brutal conditions there and this sort of got me to thinking, Jocasta, what is your purpose in life? Why did the gods place you here on this planet? Is it simply to be an interior designer? Is it really to bring happiness to people via the power of finding beautiful curtains? Or sourcing a stunning chaise longue for their study? Is that the case?'

Well Granny snorted then and put down the Blackberry that I bought her for Christmas, the one she uses mainly to check messages from her *Betfair.com* account on and barked, 'Hah! You don't even bladdy do that yourself. You get a work experience girl to do it for you.'

Mother gave Granny one of her looks and tried to

84

carry on, but at this point Kitten picked up her little Bottega Venetta handbag, rifled around in it to check something was still there, then nudged Steel and said, 'I'm off for a quick one,' and disappeared out of the door. I hoped she meant a quick pee in the loo.

'Or is my purpose in life charity work?' Mother continued, glaring at her. 'I mean, I know I've got a real knack for getting people to show up to my money-raising lunches and parties! And although I don't really like to talk about my charity work, I have done some exemplary work for, erm, Stop the Landmines and Save the Ice Caps and ... erm, ooh that one where we try and get feral children in estates to stop stabbing each other? Can't remember the name, The Children's something?'

'The Children's Revolution,' said Flash. 'That's the one that man Travis from The Jet Fighters with the funny orange hair asked you to work for in the summer when he came to your party and you were so drunk you said yes and then you were in all the papers standing next to him.'

'Yes, Flash, The Children's Revolution, thank you, darling,' Mother said beaming at him. 'So, yes, I was thinking about my charity work and then I thought, no Jocasta, the thing you contribute to the world which is more important than all of this you've missed entirely. IT'S YOUR WORK AS A MOTHER. Nothing can be more important than that. It's only as a mother that I experience such a deep amount of intense, inner joy!'

'Look, Jo, is there a point to all this?' said Daddy loudly through the laptop. 'I've got a conference call I need to take. I've got all the European CEOs on the line needing advice.'

'YES, THERE IS A POINT, JAMES!' Mummy said abruptly, using that special voice she only uses towards Daddy. 'I AM MAKING MY POINT NOW. I've been to Liberia and I've decided I'm extending the family! There will be a new arrival soon! A new Montague-Jones.'

We all looked at my mother with our mouths slightly open.

'YOU WHAT?' said Daddy frantically. 'You . . . you . . . can't be pregnant again! It's impossible!' We watched as Daddy quickly opened up his iCalender on screen and started looking at the dates. 'I've not even been in the same time zone as you, you silly woman!'

'I'm not *having* a baby, James,' shouted my mother. 'I'm *adopting* one! A little boy! From Liberia!'

'Bloody hell,' said Knute, putting his head in his hands.

'A baby, Mummy?' said Flash, looking confused. 'But, you promised that *I* was the last baby that was coming.'

I looked around the table at Granny who was laughing her head off, and Steel who seemed to be sliding down on his chair trying to disappear, and Daddy, who was right up at the screen squawking, 'Jocasta! Now you listen to me! This is absolutely NOT ON. You cannot do this without me. I forbid it!'

'Oh pipe down, James, I've done it already!' barked Mother, then she turned to me. 'Close that screen, Poppet, just shut him down, he's getting hysterical.'

'Sorry, Daddy,' I said and closed the laptop, just as Kitten appeared back in the room, seeming much more awake than when she had left,

'Right I'm back! Let's have a glass of champagne!' Kitten said. 'And what's all the shouting about?'

'Mummy is bringing a new baby from Africa,' said Flash, petulantly.

'HAHAHAHAHA!' roared Kitten. Her eyes were all wide and her left nostril was red and sore looking. 'AWESOME! Right, when is it arriving?'

'As soon as the paperwork is completed,' Mother said. 'I shall be flying back to Liberia to bring him home. He's thirteen months old.'

'A-MAAAAAZING!' said Kitten. 'The more the merrier! Get me one too! That will look awesome when I'm on the front rows in London Fashion Week! "Kitten has adopted an African!!" '

Then Kitten looked at all of our expressions and her face began to change. 'This is a joke right? Isn't it? Someone tell me it's a joke.'

'It's not a joke, Kitten!' Mother said, narrowing her eyes and sounding quite rattled. 'Maybe if you'd had some sleep in the last fortnight you'd be able to tell. Here's the news: I am adopting a Liberian orphan called Zinnah. You're getting a new little brother.'

'Zeee-naaaah?' repeated Flash. 'How do I say it again, Mummy?'

'Don't worry, Flash, I'm not calling him that,' Mother said. 'I'm naming him after the moment I first met him. When I walked into the room and he opened his mouth and cried with all his amazing teeth showing. The orphanage manageress said he was frightened as he'd never ever seen anyone with white skin ever before. He looked like a beautiful fierce little dragon. I'm calling him DRAGON. He's gorgeous.'

Well there was a silence then. A long silence. A silence that indicated that the boo-hooing was about to kick off BIG TIME.

Eventually Kitten rose up from her chair and began the altercation by saying, 'This is bloody typical! Isn't this house unbearable enough without some stranger's brat screaming in the middle of it? My head is in enough of a mess already with all these paparazzi guys chasing me and people writing crap about me and now I won't even be able to chill out and have space to be ME here. How can you be so selfish?'

Mummy just roared with angry laughter and said, 'Kitten, do spare us your self-indulgent twaddle for one moment. The whole planet doesn't revolve around you! I know this is an unfathomable concept to you! And by the way, pardon, "SPACE TO BE YOU"?! Don't talk to me about needing space. You've had so much space in the last few years to be you that you don't even know your own name any more. You're pathetic right now. PATHETIC!'

Kitten was APOPLECTIC WITH FURY then. 'There's nothing pathetic about me, Mother,' she screamed. 'I RATHER LOVE ME THANK YOU VERY MUCH! Even if no one else round here does! Look, I don't need to be here listening to your crap. Steel, get your coat we're going to Catastrophe 13 to meet Marlow and Gigi. Phone Addison Lee cars and say we need picking up ASAP.'

'Oh that's right, Kitten, scurry away back to a nightclub and drown your sorrows in bottle of champagne.' Mother said sarcastically. 'Well hear this, young lady, I'm speaking to Mr Chenowitz the accountant in the morning, first thing, and I'm making a legal bid to get your trust fund SUSPENDED! I've good reason to believe you're spending it on drugs.'

As soon as the word 'drugs' was mentioned things got really messy. Kitten started getting up in *my* face being aggressive and accusing me of 'making up lies' about her, as usual, like the little brat I bloody am! Then Mummy told Kitten that she was tired of her being 'out of control' and 'she was being forced towards some extreme measures' (whatever that meant), meanwhile the waiting staff from Chosen Leaf tidied up plates around us all pretending to be deaf. Suddenly, I remembered Flash, who was looking really tired what with it being nearly eleven o'clock, and I took him upstairs to hand him to Marcella, his night-time nanny, to put him in his pyjamas for bed.

I was seriously hoping Flash had missed some of the worst parts of what had been said, but as I was kissing him goodnight he looked up at me with big wide eyes and said, 'Poppet, is Mummy really getting a new baby?'

'Oh . . . oh, I don't know, Flash,' I said. 'It could be one of Mummy's mad plans. She may forget about it again soon. Don't worry.'

And then Flash said, 'Is Kitten really on drugs?'

'Oh . . . oh, I don't know. Don't think about that now it's not nice. I'm not going to. Let's just think about happy things.'

Then I came up to my bedroom. All I could hear downstairs was tonnes of shouting and door-slamming so I got into bed and put in my ear plugs and put on an eyemask and took half of the Diazepam sleeping pill that mother gave me the last time I flew long-haul to the Hamptons in America. Then I wrapped myself up in my duvet like a sausage roll and I tried to think of happy things and soon I was out cold.

SATURDAY 26TH SEPTEMBER

Something pretty ginormous happened at 1 Octavia Square tonight and I want to write it down here in my own words so I can talk about it with Dr Sarzberg. He was right about writing things down being really helpful for understanding stuff. It is. Especially when your family is written about in the newspapers all the time like mine is, it's bloody impossible to remember what really happened in your life and what was an exaggeration and what was a total lie made up by someone who needed some money.

Like, for example, earlier this month on the night of the 'lovely dinner', Mummy did NOT threaten Kitten with a knife. And there WASN'T a food fight involving the entire family including Granny. This didn't ruddy happen at all, although it was on pages 6 and 7 of the *Sun*. They said that my mother and Kitten were in the kitchen and my mother was waving a knife. THIS DID NOT HAPPEN. I mean, yes, OK, Kitten and Mother had a screaming row about the adopting a baby thing (that's never been mentioned since, thank God), but the whole knife thing was just utter CRAP that one of the staff from Chosen Leaf just made up and sold to the *Sun*. A reporter rang Mother up the next morning to ask if it was true and Mother's eyes went all wide and mental and bulging like they do when she's just had fresh Botox and she screeched, 'Of course it bloody isn't!! It's a load of absolute bleeping bleepy-bleep POPPYCOCK! My family aren't savages!' (She didn't say 'bleep' she said much worse things I don't want to write.)

Anyway, the *Sun* reporter just printed the story anyway and it took up two whole pages and there were pictures of Kitten doing high kicks on the tables at Catastrophe 13 later that night with the gusset of her knickers showing and her eyes closed, plus quotes from 'sources close to

Kitten' who claimed she was 'deeply shaken by the incident involving a twelve inch Sabatier blade.'

Oh my God, it was so embarrassing.

And if this wasn't HIDEOUS enough, about two days later a ruddy policeman came to the door and said he needed to investigate 'an alleged violent incident'. And by this point my mother looked like she might actually punch him smack down the steps back into the square but Knute managed to calm her by escorting her into the drawing room and doing some transcendental meditation breathing. Then Kitten, who'd just got out of the shower, floated downstairs with wet hair wearing a little flimsy Sonia Rykiel star print T-shirt dress with no bra, being all sweet and charming like she can be and said, 'Honestly officer this is all a silly misunderstanding. It's just a made up story by someone who wants to make money.'

'Sorry, love, I know. I'm just doing my job. I'll say no more about it,' said the officer, then he asked Kitten for her autograph for his little girl and left.

I sat on the staircase outside the living-room, glowering my best DEATH STARE OF SATAN at him as he went. I was TOTALLY FUMING and wanting to scream, 'Say no more about it? The whole of bloody Britain has been talking about it! And it didn't even happen!'

After the knife story I phoned Mother's assistant Matthew, which was quite bolshy of me, but I feel quite bolshy these days, and I said I was sick of people coming into our house to deliver food and stuff if they were going to be so horrid. In fact no more strangers in the house FULL STOP.

'Look, Pop, people have been fired at Chosen Leaf about that story, believe me,' said Matthew. 'But I have to warn you, this sort of thing is going to happen now and again. Kitten is making you into a very famous family and people are interested in you all, so we just have to try to be extra-careful about who we speak to, right? People are vultures, Poppet. They'll sell any little bit of tittle-tattle for a hundred quid. It's just a matter of working out who we can trust.'

It made me feel sad when he said that. Why does anyone want to be famous if this is what it's like?

Anyway, just as we got past that FIASCO, well tonight ruddy happened, which means the Montague-Jones family will be back in the *Sun* again. So before I forget the truth this is what really occurred:

Tonight Felix and I went to Jackdaw's party at Voyage together. Striker decided we should all take dates to the party, so at 8pm I walked across to Felix's through the communal gardens as he said he would get us a lift there. I walked to Felix's in bare feet carrying my shoes as I totally can't walk in high heels, I can only stand up or sit down. I've not built 'moving about' into my repertoire although it's certainly something else to add to my

Things To Achieve list along with learning to wear foundation and learning how to put on false eyelashes without glueing my eyelids shut and requiring a BUPA emergency ambulance.

Anyway, it was 8pm and I was late. I said I'd be there at 7.15 but I'd been faffing about for hours with what to wear, getting all freaked out. I'd settled on a black strappy dress with a ruffly pink tutu petticoat, pale green shoes and dark red feathers in my hair.

To be honest the whole thing was a lot more girly-whirly-shmirly 'Ooooh look at me!' than usual and I was feeling sort of paranoid. I was glad I'd bought my little crocheted cardigan as in the twilight my blotchy upper arms reminded me of when Mrs Minsk boils a ham in berries at Christmas and leaves it on the kitchen side and you have to stare at it for ages to work out whether it's ham, beef or some weird space meat that's just been invented, ie: ruddy gross.

Thank God me and Felix were going to the party together as he always cheers me up. Not boyfriend and girlfriend 'together'. Just together like Felix and I do. Just kicking about. Obviously, everyone at Lycée assumes there's something totally filthy going on between me and Felix Hayes-Burlington from Godspeed Academy Year Eleven, and imagines every time I'm in his bedroom it's because we're nude and jumping off wardrobes having mad passionate sessions, but that's simply not true. We're completely, always not. Most of the time we're playing

Hungry Hippos and eating jam on toast or sitting looking at laptops sending each other links to laugh at.

So I got to Felix's and clacked on the front door for what seemed like ages using the ancient brass door-clacker that no one in his family can ever hear, but Felix's father Dr Hayes-Burlington insists on keeping it as he hates modern doorbells. Actually Dr H-B loathes almost everything about modern life – radiators, electricity, computers, antibiotics – and he seriously believes the world was a jollier place when everyone sat in freezing houses, dying of smallpox, reading ruddy dull nine-hundred page Charles Dickens novels by candlelight and doing poos in china bowls kept under the beds as there was no inside loo. GREAT TIMES!

By the way, I'm not being bitchy about Dr H-B, I think he's actually rather amazing even if he is as nutty as a bag of frogs. Both Felix's parents are legends. They're both Professors of English Literature at University College London and I've never worked out exactly what that means they do but I know it involves Felix's dad wearing brown tweed jackets with grey corduroy patches on the elbows, trousers that are always at least ten centimetres too short, having mad hair and carrying piles of papers around while sighing.

Felix's mother wears a long black cape and she cycles from Hampstead to Bloomsbury each day on an ancient bike with a shopping basket full of books on the front and she's always flying off to Vienna or somewhere at a moment's notice to examine a dictionary that someone's discovered in a loft.

Oh, and Felix's parents have this totally MAD belief, which I can't get my head around, that, 'It's not fair to make other people clean your house if you're able bodied' so they don't have a cleaner! In fact they don't HAVE ANY STAFF AT ALL! They just sort of do things on their own! They don't even have, like, a Mrs Minsk, who knows how to change toilet rolls and or what to do if you run out of food or someone spills something on the carpet. That is totally headbending. I do love hanging out at Felix's house though, even if I always have to take an antihistamine pill if I'm going round there as it's so dusty I end up sneezing till I'm sick.

There's something about being with Felix that makes me feel, like, totally safe.

So after a whole lot of clacking and banging Felix appeared at the door. He looked down at me, as he's about 5 foot 11 tall and makes me feel like a pipsqueak, and he said, 'Christ, Poppet, you look amazing.' Then he kissed me on both cheeks. The patches behind his ears smelled of lovely Miller Harris aftershave and Aveda hair wax. He was wearing a black blazer jacket with the collar half pulled up and half wonky; a white, tight-fitting button up shirt, skinny grey jeans and bright white slip-on yacht shoes. His nearly blond hair was, as it ever is with Felix, sort of spiky in places and floppy on the fringe, like four hairstyles battling with each other at once.

Felix's eyes looked especially green tonight and his lips girlishly full. Felix is sort of a girlish type of boy, but I can assure people he's very much a boy all the same.

'Oh gngngng, Felix, I don't. I look DISGUSTING,' I sighed. I was feeling all hot and bothered.

Am I the only girl in Britain who feels like this before they go out? Everyone else is like HONK HONK WOOO PARTY! Like when Striker starts getting ready for parties she texts you the minute she's dressed and says, 'DAMN IT POPS I LOOK HAAAAWWWT, I want to stay home and MOLEST MYSELF.'

And Vixen, well she just sort of wanders into her big sister Frangipan's room and picks any old dress, throws it on, sticks a ribbon in her hair and sits on the couch calmly waiting for her lift looking like the prettiest girl in London.

'I've been looking at myself in the mirror,' I announced to Felix, as we stood in his hallway, 'and I've decided that I look like an orangutan. An orangutan on its birthday. And all the other orangutangs have chipped in to buy me a sack to wear to look fancy.'

'You don't look like an orangutan,' Felix sighed. 'You look amazing. Like, WOW! What a pair!' Felix said pointing to my boobs and making his eyes go all swirly.

'These?!' I said, looking down at them. 'Oh don't get excited, Flux, they're not real. Go on, have a feel if you want.' I pushed my chest out towards him, 'I've just pushed the piles of nothing together with a good bra and the rest is those 34D Rigby and Peller cleavage enhancer chicken fillet pads. And they're beginning to get all moist and sweaty underneath already. It's all fake.'

'Oh, Pop, do stop this filthy talk,' Felix sighed, shaking his head. 'I'm getting all overexcited.' We both laughed. I knew I was acting a bit mad, but it's OK as Felix doesn't mind me being mad.

'I've lost my damned credit card,' Felix said as we walked up the spiral staircase's dark red velvety carpets, holding the dark brown bannisters, past the antique chairs on every stairwell piled up high with dusty books and manuscripts. On the third floor there's a stuffed lion's head I always stop to stare at. It's a lion's head mounted, mid-growl, on a plaque with a tribute below that says:

KENYA. AUGUST 14TH 1921 – A MAGNIFICENT DAY

FOR THE BURLINGTON FAMILY

And I always look at it and think, Yeah, magnificent day for YOU GUYS, not such a ruddy good day for the poor lion who was just popping out for some lunch and got a bullet in his ass. I've told Felix this and he totally agrees.

Me and Felix agree on almost everything.

In Felix's room on the top floor I lay down on his enormous king-sized bed and picked up his spare MacBook and started clicking through online gossip columns. Felix was crawling around under the bed looking for his Coutts card which would have been really bloody heavy if he'd lost it as it's got a limit on it of about two hundred grand.

Felix is sort of lucky like I am about money as his great-grandfather was Jarvis J Burlington the famous crime novel author whose books are always getting made into Hollywood movies and translated into practically every language on earth. So Felix's family are quite comfortable.

Striker says I should definitely marry Felix as soon as possible as the Hayes-Burlington family are even richer than the Montague-Jones family and both our trust funds together would make me, like, richer than the Queen or something. But I always tell Striker I don't really care about that sort of crap. In fact the more I think about it over the last few weeks I don't care about money at all. It's only bloody money.

'Any more stabbings at your house then?' Felix shouted from under the bed as I lay above reading TMZ.com gossip about how my sister Kitten and that guy Steel Drum have split up, but rumours have it that Kitten is dating another boy who looks a bit like Steel Drum but it's not him it's 'Farrow Cordell', though 'sources close to Kitten' say that they're worried about the young socialite as, since her alleged affair with married movie star Brandon Gissamo, she's been partying much harder than usual and has been spotted with bruises on her body especially on her arms . . .' That was exactly the point I decided to close the laptop and pass it off in my head as untrue.

'FELIX! THERE NEVER WAS A KNIFE!' I said, although I knew he was only winding me up.

'IT'S HERE! I've got the card. Thank God!' shouted Felix. 'OK, come on, let's go to Voyage and show face at Jackdaw's stupid party.'

We ran out of the house and jumped into the back of the Mercedes Benz waiting outside on the kerb for us and set off to Chelsea.

All the while Striker was on my Blackberry, quacking in my ear, 'WHERRRRE ARE YOU POPPSHET?! IS FELIX WITH YOU OR WHAT? HURRY YOUR ARSES UP!' She was laughing about the bar staff at Voyage who were being totally slack about proof of age IDs, so she'd had three shots of tequila poured down her throat by a man wearing just silver swimming trunks already. Striker said she'd already dumped that boy, Peche, from Winchester Boys' School who was supposed to be her date as he was a complete wet fart who kept droning on about playing rugby and telling her that tequila was 'no drink for a lady'.

Striker said she'd told him not to speak to her any more and go and stand somewhere else. Striker said Vixen was already in Voyage too and she'd done the red carpet with Jackdaw Penry and everyone was saying they made a really, really hot couple and Vixen was wearing an incredible leopard-print dress that you could see her thong through in strong light and the paparazzi were going insane. Striker said her and Vixen had managed to get photographed together and it was almost definitely going to be in the party section in *Vogue*.

'And that, Popshypie,' shouted Striker, 'is pretty much as bloody good as life gets!'

'What's she saying?' Felix said to me, poking my knee.

'She's drunk,' I mouthed to Felix.

'Brilliant,' sighed Felix, and neither of us said anything for a while. We both know how Striker can be a bit of a handful when she's been drinking.

To be honest, I was worrying she'd do something really mental like she did at Lady Iris's sleepover this summer where we were all meant to be sleeping in tents in the garden and drinking non-alcoholic cocktails but Striker sneaked a bottle of Glenlivet whisky there in her bag and got rat-arsed and ended up INSIDE the house, inside the bedroom of Lady Iris's eighteen-year-old big brother, Rufus, who is a legendary ladies man.

Then someone, I think it was the Right Honourable Petronella grassed Striker up to Lady Iris's mother and things got really messy and Striker's mum Paloma was telephoned in the middle of the night and ordered to take Striker home.

'Your child is a complete MONSTER!' Lady Iris's mother was screaming at Paloma in the street.

And Paloma was shouting back in her brilliant Spanish accent, 'She's a fourteen-year-old girl! Your son is a filthy pig! I'll call the police and tell them he's a paedophile and make them chop it off!'

That was sort of heavy. And the following month was quite worrying for everyone involved too.

I'm starting to think Striker is maybe one of those people, like my Uncle Augustus, Mother's brother, who shouldn't be allowed to drink at all. Not even a tiny drop.

Augustus has got an illness where he loves it so much he can't stop and it sends him peculiar in the head. Augustus didn't even know he had this illness until he was about thirty, when he was drinking like a litre of vodka for breakfast and he bet his entire mansion in a poker game and ending up living in a Volvo estate car behind a shopping centre in Shepherds Bush. He was in a right old mess. He had no money left at all and he was living on free soup from the church and washing his face and bits in the sinks in the shopping centre toilets and Aunt Serendipity divorced him and starting having sex with their gardener. It was sort of heavy.

The weird thing is, everyone says that until all the bad stuff happened Uncle Augustus was the best laugh EVER and always the last one to leave any party. That's what worries me about booze. It seems to sort of make people amazingly happy for a bit, but for some people it also makes them end up homeless and want to be dead.

Anyway, we got to Voyage and the road was blocked with cars and limos dropping people off, so we jumped out on the corner of the block and walked.

Felix and I were on the 'VVVIP' list so we didn't have to queue but when we tried to slip through the crowds to the front doors, a tiny blonde woman with a clipboard and a headset spotted me and yelled, 'You're Poppet Montague-Jones aren't you?'

'Erm, yeah,' I said.

'This way please then.' She grabbed me by the arm and dragged me over to the red carpet entrance and said, 'Could you just pose for some photos in front of the sponsor's boards?' She pointed at the display which read, 'Gran Patron Tequila sponsors Penry Yachting.'

'Ooh, erm OK,' I mumbled. I didn't feel like I had much choice to be honest and I know these type of photos make my mother really happy.

So I tried to look all normal and put my arms over my boobs and the woman shouted to all the paparazzi guys, 'Kitten Montague-Jones' little sister!'

And right away the pack of men wth cameras all went mad shouting, 'Kitten's sister!' Kitten's sister! And some of them were just shouting 'Kitten' as if it didn't matter that they were actually speaking to the wrong one.

'Turn round and look over your shoulder, be a bit sexy sweetheart, let us see you from behind, be a good girl,' shouted one man. Another guy seemed to put the camera down low as if he was almost trying to take a photo up my skirt, so I jumped backwards and clamped my legs tight shut.

I hate having my picture taken if I'm honest. If anyone

tags me on Bebo or Facebook I just take the tags right off because I hate how I look, which is hideous. Like my skin is made out of a different substance to everyone else's, like Vixen is made from silk and I'm made from porridge. And I never smile, for obvious reasons.

Anyway, I stood there blinking in all the flashing bulbs and eventually Felix realized how ruddy awkward I was and he stomped over saying, 'Oh come on, Poppet, they've got enough now,' then pulled me away. The woman with the clipboard didn't say thank you or goodbye or anything, she just ticked my name off on a clipboard then looked through me like I didn't exist any more. By the time we got into the party and started searching for the VVVIP room it was well past ten o'clock.

To get inside the VVVIP room you needed a special platinum and gold wristband and the guest list had been specially chosen by Jackdaw Penry's dad, Balthazar, so it really felt like we were some of the 'chosen few' at this party. Mr Penry is this tall, intimidating guy with a bald head and a deep brown mahogany tan whose photo is always in *The Times* in the finance section standing beside one of his yachts smoking a cigar and giving advice on how to hide your savings in other countries so you don't have to pay full tax on it here. Mr Penry is a bit of a legend really amongst Godspeed Academy boys. They all want to grow up and be like him and have loads of money and ex-wives and yachts and go on holiday with Richard Branson on Necker Island and crap like that.

Personally I don't care about all the Very Important Person and Very Very Important Person stuff, but Mother says when I go to nightclubs I should always find the VIP part as soon as possible and stay there as the normal rooms can have some extremely dodgy people in there indeed. And most of these normal people don't know how to behave and some of them don't smell good either so it's best to steer clear. Mother says life is too bloody short to spend around ordinary people in high street clothes made of flammable fibres and if I ever have to go to the loo in such places I should lay down a layer of toilet roll around the loo seat so my bum cheeks don't catch scabies. In fact one time Mother even tried to teach me a yoga move so I could squat with my ass cheeks an inch above the loo seat 'allowing me to hover confidently while my muscles could still let urine leave the uterus'. Oh my God that was embarrassing. My mother is totally famous for having NO SENSE of appropriate mother/daughter conversation. This yoga/urine incident was almost as bad as two years ago when I got my first period and I was hiding in the bathroom trying to come to terms with the gunge that had appeared in my knickers, wanting some privacy, and my mother was BANGING ON THE DOOR waving a tampon offering to PUT IT IN FOR ME!!

Yes, THIS REALLY HAPPENED. I still have panic attacks about the thought of my mother's face squashed against the frosted glass brandishing a Tampax

Lite, quacking, 'Poppet, I gave birth to you! I've seen your vagina on many occasions. You came out of mine! It's no big deal! Let me in, I can make sure it's inserted properly and then we can go and celebrate. I've called Pearl, she's bringing Jemima, we're going to Harvey Nichols to have sushi for lunch to celebrate!'

I am DEFINITELY telling Dr Sarzberg about this incident as it's something I will take with me to my grave.

Anyway, as we were getting our VVVIP bands everyone in the VVIP room was staring at Felix and me. Then a really angry-looking girl who hadn't got a VVVIP band said loudly, 'Who the hell do those two think they are? She's only some bloody drug addict's little sister! She's nobody!'

I wanted to turn around and say, 'I don't think I'm anyone! Nobody at all!' But thankfully I managed to stay quiet. Inside the VVVIP room it was basically a small dark dance-floor with about one hundred people standing around it and a few people dancing to bad house music. And I mean BAD. Like that cheesy crap my father puts on his iPod when he gets home from playing poker and he's had a few brandies and he starts waving his hands in the air and trying to convince us he used to go to illegal warehouse parties before we were born, which MUST BE A LIE as we can't even put Capital FM on in the kitchen these days without him boo-hooing and sticking on *Gardener's Question Time* on BBC Radio 4 instead.

NB: HE DOESN'T EVEN LIKE GARDENING! HE JUST FEELS SAFER WHEN RADIO 4 IS ON AND IT'S OLD PEOPLE TALKING ABOUT SOIL.

I looked around the crowd in the VVVIP room and realized that aside from Jacob, Vix, Livvy, Bettina, and some other friends, this place was mostly full of twenty-year-old fashion models, old guys (at least thirty-five years old) and practically naked waiters and waitresses carrying trays of tequila.

As we walked through the crowd Felix took a tequila then chucked it to the back of his throat which looked sort of manly, until he made a face like he was going to projectile puke it down my front immediately, then he looked at me holding my little glass that I'd been given and he said, 'Poppet, I'm not sure you're supposed to be drinking are you?'

I looked at him and thought, 'you know something, Felix, I don't know. I'm not sure what the rules are in my house anymore. Because I can drink champagne with Granny. And wine at dinner if we're in Tuscany. And I steal Knute's beers from the fridge now and again and no one notices, and my big sister Kitten is a drug addict and an alcoholic, so in the grand scheme of things a tiny little tequila seems fine. In fact, to be honest, being numb sort of makes me feel better.

But I didn't want to bother Felix with all this stuff so I just said, 'Oh whatever! Down the hatch!' like Granny says, then I chucked it down my throat. Obviously about a second later I remembered that tequila tastes like the bleach Mrs Minsk sterilizes the bottom of our kitchen bin with and my eyes started to water and I felt like someone had punched me in the forehead.

Tequila is vile. VILE! I wish I was allowed to say this out loud but Blitzen and Amelia at school always go on about how it's their favourite drink ever so we all have to agree.

As I walked up to Vixen she grabbed me and hugged me and kissed me on both cheeks but I could tell she was quite stressed. Jackdaw, who was beside her, didn't look too happy either. My gut instinct right then told me it was something to do with Striker, although this doesn't exactly make me a psychic. It's always to do with bloody Striker.

'Oh, Poppet, thank God you're here! I'd nearly given up. It's quarter past ten!' Vix said. 'Jesus, you look amazing. You look like Lindsay Lohan!'

'Yeah, right,' I groaned. 'Where's Striker?'

'Err, well, yeah,' Vixen sighed. 'She's a bit, well, messy. She sort of got into a fight with Peche by calling him a Winchester School bedwetter, so then they had quite a loud argument by the bar, then she was dancing, but nobody else was so she was trying to drag people on to the dance floor and yelling "NO FUN" at them when they wouldn't dance!'

'Oh dear God,' I said.

'And last time we saw her she was over by the

bar hassling the bartender to make her a cocktail with absinthe.'

'Oh heavens above,' I said. 'That's so not good is it?'

'Well, maybe I'm being over the top, Poppet?' said Vixen. 'I mean some people think she's quite funny. But Jacob's getting majorly stressed as he was only allowed a guestlist as long as we all behaved. So I told her to calm down as Mr Penry was beginning to notice her and freak out about how underage she was, but Strikes told me to stop nagging her and then she dropped a drink on my foot and I don't know what to do now, Poppet. I really don't know what to do.'

Vixen looked at me with her usual wide, helpless eyes like I might know what to do, but I totally didn't know what to do at all, so I did what I always do in such circumstances, I asked Felix. Felix always knows what to do.

Felix was chatting with Marmaduke Adams, so I tapped him on the shoulder and said I had a situation. Marmaduke was trying to catch my eye as if to say hello but I just ignored him. Why does Marmaduke want to say hello to me, the complete freak? He hates me!

I whispered into Felix's ear what I knew about Striker and he thought for a second and said, 'OK, why don't we find Striker first and we can suss out the damage?' I rang Striker a few times but it went straight to voicemail which is basically just her screaming 'Hello! Hello!' in a really bizarre voice which is a complete freak-out the first time you hear it as it sounds like you've interrupted her getting murdered.

So anyway, Felix, Vixen and I set off around the club snooping around all of the bars and alcoves and dance-floors in search of a small woman with newly-dyed jet-black short hair and huge knockers wearing a multi-coloured Stella McCartney baby doll dress that Vixen said made her look like a 'sexy peacock'.

After half an hour Striker was absolutely nowhere to be seen. Finally, after an hour, I walked into the third floor ladies loos and the search got a little more successful.

As I walked in, one of those ladies who gives out the hand towels and perfume was bashing on a door with her fist shouting, 'Hello!! Open the door!! You been in there far too long now. What is going on?'

Then I heard a voice groan, 'Oh bloody leave me alone! I'm haaaving a sit-down you stupid woman!'

I could tell right away it was Striker.

'Striker,' I said, walking up and banging the door with my hand. 'It's Poppet! Open the door and let me in right now!'

Well this must have given Striker a complete jolt because the door bolt shuddered almost immediately and Striker put her head round the door about halfway down and said, 'Poppet? Ooh it's you! Come in!'

I slid through the gap in the door into the cubicle. Striker was sitting on the loo, with her thong around her ankles, looking up at me with messy eye-makeup and a shiny face. She looked a bit frazzled.

'Hey, Striker,' I said. 'Having a good time?'

Striker looked at me and then she wrinkled her nose and beckoned me closer.

'I have a secret to tell you,' she whispered,

'Right,' I whispered back.

'Don't drink the tequila,' she said. 'It's got poison in it. I drank some of it. That's why I'm sitting down as I have been taken over by a terrible malady.'

'I see,' I nodded.

'And it also contains truth serum too,' she said. 'I told Peche that his breath smells of old man's farts.' Striker burped, then put her hand to her mouth. 'I am naughty aren't I?'

'You're a very naughty girl, Striker,' I said.

Striker was a little bit drunk. But to be honest, on the Striker Earhart scale of things I was quite relieved by what I was seeing. She was still chatty and awake and making sense. My biggest worry was that she might not be able to stand up properly and then I'd have to pull her bloody knickers up like I did after Livvy's parents' summer barbecue when Striker conned one of the adults into letting her drink the punch. Pulling someone's pants up for them is NOT easy. Especially if they keep falling over and bringing you down with them.

'Do you want to go home, Strikes?' I said.

Striker thought about this and then she said, 'Well I

111

suppose we should. It's very very late isn't it? Has the club closed?'

'Oh, yes,' I lied, but it was a white lie for her own good. 'It's time for us all to go home.'

'Right you are, then,' she said. 'Give me a hand to pull me up.'

I pulled Striker upright and made sure her pants were at a correct functional level for walking. Then I got out my phone and called for a car to pick us up. I didn't think it was right to send Striker home in a cab alone. I think you should always make sure your friends get safely home.

And to be quite honest I thought Jackdaw's party sort of sucked. It was sort of fake and full of boring plastic people. I can't work out why Kitten likes these bloody party things. She sometimes goes to two or three or even four of them a night! And she always always does the red carpet picture thing where the horrible men call her 'love' and take pictures of her bum. Kitten loves doing red carpet! And Knute and Mother and Granny always do it when they're asked too. Sometimes I think I'm from a totally different DNA pool to my family. I don't even look like any of them. They're all tall and long limbed and fair skinned and I'm short and ball-like and translucent with blue veins.

Felix and I left Voyage at eleven-thirty, with our arms through Striker's arms, propping her up, and jumped into the back of the black Volkswagen people-carrier waiting for us.

We'd almost reached the corner of the Kings Road before the voice in the driver's seat said, 'So back to the home address? Octavia Square, Poppet?' And that's when I realized it was Cyril.

'Oh, yes please, Cyril! Thank you, amazing. How are you?'

'Oh you know me, Poppet,' he said. 'Just driving around here and there. Staying out of trouble. You just sit back and relax now and I'll get you kids safely home.'

There was something so lovely about the way Cyril said that, that it made me want to cry.

So we set off back all the way across London from Chelsea to Hampstead again with Striker's head on my knee, fast asleep snoring, and my head on Felix's shoulder, both of us singing along to Magic FM which was playing ancient love songs from the 1990s that somehow we both knew all the words to.

This was definitely the very best part of the night.

When we delivered Striker back to her front door it was just on half past midnight and she tottered quite normally up the steps to her front door and was home before her curfew time. Felix and I high-fived each other and agreed that this was a good thing that we'd both done.

I looked into Felix's eyes and he looked into mine. We didn't say anything. It was a lovely clear night with tonnes of stars in the sky and a big almost full moon shining up there.

'Fancy a pot of tea?' he finally said. So we went back arm in arm to his house to drink our usual gallon of Earl Grey tea and we were chatting and laughing so much as we went that I didn't notice my own house and the drama happening there at all.

Felix and I went upstairs and lay on his bed slurping tea, trying to see if we could fit two extra-chunky Fortnum and Mason chocolatey biscuits in our mouths at once and laughing at stupid clips on YouTube. Felix was trying to explain to me about space and light years and how far away the stars we can see from his skylight are. And I was telling him about Deathbreath Douglas and Granny's Picasso, and we were both giggling like crazy and at one point I thought we were going to choke with laughter. Then I lay down on the bed properly and kicked my shoes off and Felix kicked his off and we lay side by side staring at the ceiling like we used to do when we were little but we don't do as much now we're grown up.

Felix put out his hand and put it around mine and we lay holding hands, touching each other's fingers and wrestling our toes and saying nothing for a while.

Then I turned my face towards his and said, 'So do you want to try again maybe?'

Felix looked at me and said, 'Well I suppose so, yes.'

'OK then, me too,' I said.

So I closed my eyes and Felix kissed me on the lips. First with our mouths closed, just softly on my lips, and then with our mouths open with tongues, but not too much tongue because of my brace. We carried on snogging for about half a minute and then Felix's hand slid down my side and slid on to my waist and round my back and felt my bum, but then we stopped. We both opened our eyes and looked at each other.

'Still nothing?' Felix said. I thought for a little bit.

'Not really,' I said. 'What about you?'

'Erm, a bit weird,' he said. 'I mean, better than last time. But still sort of like kissing my friend.'

'I know,' I said. 'Me too.'

Then we didn't say anything for ages again. We were both trying to work out what was going on. We just lay there in silence in Felix's totally silent house with the skylight open and this is when we could hear the drama over the road at my house when it reached its peak. Front doors slamming, people screaming, mopeds revving, car horns honking. The sound of a woman crying. Felix and I jumped up and got up on chairs and poked our heads out to see what was going on.

From high above Octavia Square I could clearly see Daddy standing on the front doorstep of our house. He was wearing a dressing gown looking really upset, but really angry too. Dr Sarzberg the therapist was with him holding a briefcase. Dr Sarzberg was passing Daddy some pieces of paper. There was three or four other people dressed quite normally in jeans and jackets who seemed to be just loitering about waiting for someone. There was more than the usual number of paparazzi guys buzzing about on mopeds causing a nuisance and lots of the neighbours' cleaners and housekeepers were standing on their doorsteps watching our house like they were waiting for a show. Eventually the front door opened and out walked a tiny little figure holding a pillow and a small overnight suitcase. It was Kitten.

She was wearing a gold dress, a trilby hat and her feet were bare. When Kitten appeared, the people in jeans and jackets sort of encircled her, not in a threatening way, but like they were protecting her. They walked her to a Vauxhall estate car and Kitten very calmly got in the back seat and the doors closed and the car drove off. It was rather undramatic really. Just sad and very upsetting.

I mean, obviously, by the time everyone reads about it in the *Sun* it will sound much more exciting and reporters will say that Kitten screeched and punched people and had to wear a strait-jacket, but the truth is that by the time Kitten left Octavia Square she was in such a mess with her drug addiction that she didn't have the energy to make her feelings truly known to anyone.

And that's why even though my heart is broken about it I'm glad my big sister Kitten has been finally sent to rehab.

OCTOBER

SATURDAY 2ND OCTOBER

Mother says the rule is we're not allowed to see Kitten.

No visits to Paradise Vision Rehabilitation Centre whatsoever. That's the rules. The 'tough love' method – that's what Dr Sarzberg calls it. That means that absolutely everyone in the addict's life cuts themselves off until they see the error of their ways and 'want to change'.

I don't quite see it myself. My big sister has spent every day for the past two years telling me to 'shut up and leave her alone'. In fact, one time when she said this last year I actually lost it and attacked her with a tennis racket and she started screaming and picked up a hockey stick and we were both basically rolling around on the fourth floor landing beating each other about the face and legs with sports equipment until Knute dragged Kitten away and actually locked her in her room.

I think that day possibly goes down as a very LOW point in Montague-Jones family history. That's what we would have had written on the plaque on the wall if one of us had died during the battle and we'd just kept the head as a trophy.

I don't know what happened really. She just told me to shut-up for the hundreth time that week and a red mist sort of descended around my eyes and next thing I knew I was trying to give her hair a centre parting with a K Blade junior team racket.

And now she's in rehab and we're meant to be helping her by not speaking to her.

How? How can letting Kitten get her own way AGAIN help her out!?

'It's what Dr Sarzberg wants!' Mother yelled at me this morning as we were eating breakfast. Well, I was eating porridge that Mrs Minsk had made me, Mother was drinking a protein shake that was green and smelled like farts and feet and seemed to have lumps of twig floating in it. She says it helps her experience 'deeper joy during her ashtanga yoga squats'.

'Mother,' I said. 'Why do we always listen to Dr Sarzberg? Why can't we just make our own minds up about what we think about this situation?'

Mother seemed to be pretending to be deaf.

'Flash thinks,' I continued, 'that Dr Sarzberg isn't even a proper doctor. Flash got into an argument with Dr Sarzberg last week because Flash pointed out that the medical certificates on his wall looked like he'd made them himself using Microsoft Windows! Flash says the certificates are from universities in countries that don't even exist!'

My mother rolled her eyes. 'Oh Flash says all sorts of things to get attention,' she tutted. 'Just ignore him. That's why *he's* in therapy.'

I stared at her for a minute. It's starting to dawn on me lately that my mother says some pretty dumb things. And I seem to be more in a place these days where I want to argue with her about them too. It's freaking me out because this is what happened with Kitten and Mother back when Kitten was in Year Eleven. Well not that she finished Year Eleven. She was thrown out of her boarding school long before the GCSEs and Hampstead Lycée asked her to leave in Year Nine.

But the point is, that once upon a time Mother and Kitten were pretty good friends. In fact Kitten was definitely the favourite.

'Maybe Flash is lying so much, BECAUSE we ignore him,' I said to Mother. Mother's eyes narrowed when I said that.

'Don't be ridiculous!' she said. 'No! They think Flash might have ADHD or bipolar or high-functioning Asperger's or something. That's why they're testing him.'

I just shook my head. There is nothing wrong with little Flash. Flash is perfect. I love him. He's just a lot smarter than all of us and none of us know what to do with him. He's got some strong ideas himself though. In fact, Blitzen Trapper told me the other day that her father found a letter pushed through the gate on their house in Bishops Avenue last week and when he opened it, it was from Flash. Flash had sent Mr Trapper his CV asking him for work experience at Trapper Aerospace helping Blitzen's father develop bombs and guns! He'd even sent a covering letter listing all the reasons why he'd be good at it. HE IS SIX YEARS OLD.

'OK, then,' I said to Mother. 'What if I just sent a little email to the receptionists at the rehab place? And they could pass it to Kitten?'

'No!' said Mother. 'Look, Poppet, this rehab is costing me a ruddy arm and leg! I need it to be over *très très VITE*! I can't even leave the bloody country to do my interior design work in New York because of this. The rehab clinic have requested that I stay close by in London in case of an emergency! I'm losing important clients left, right and centre over this fiasco!' Mother picked up some wallpaper and carpet samples off the kitchen work surface and stuffed them in her handbag. 'Kitten has got to be cured by the end of October or my schedules are screwed!' she said.

I must have looked a bit tearful when Mummy said that, as she put her hand on my shoulder and said, 'Look, Poppet, don't fret, they've got some brilliant therapists at Paradise Vision. Surely they can get to the bottom of Kitten's problems can't they? All this constant attention-seeking? It's gone on too long.' As she said this, she picked up her Blackberry and walked off checking her emails.

'But I don't see how a Get Well card would harm Kitten,' I mumbled under my breath. I'd been planning to try to make Kitten smile by sending her a card made from potato prints, just like we used to do together when we were little. When Mother was away, Mrs Minsk used to keep us entertained by helping us cut a potato in half and make it into a star or a moon shape, then she'd sellotape big sheets of paper to the kitchen table downstairs and make us 'paint' from mixed up flour and water with food colouring in it, then we'd splodge the mess all over the place and make silly paintings. It was the best fun ever. Mummy used to say the potato-print paintings were silly and didn't make sense but Mrs M used to love them and stick them up in her little flat on her fridge, so they couldn't have been that crap.

'No Get Well cards either!' Mother said. I gave her my best killer scowl of doom. I was starting to get rather angry. I'm annoyed enough that I was left out of the plan to stage an 'intervention' on Kitten as it is. That's what they call it when your family all gang together in a united front to make you go to rehab. It's quite sneaky really. The addict doesn't know it's going to happen. It's like an ambush.

In Kitten's case Knute fooled Kitten into dropping by the house to have her photo taken with him for *Star!* magazine for a story about 'Britain's Most Celebtastic Brothers and Sisters'. Except Knute was lying. There was no photo shoot. But Kitten totally fell for it and she showed, admittedly an hour late, and was faced with Mother, Father, Knute, Granny, Mrs Minsk, Uncle Augustus and Steel Drum all camped in the living-room waiting to embroil her in a massive 'Let's Slag Kitten Off' session.

Everyone decided beforehand that I was far too young to be involved. I'm actually rather LIVID about that. I don't think they think I'm too young. I think they think I'm an idiot.

Well, apparently the intervention went on for ages and Kitten was sobbing and Uncle Augustus said some very heavy things about how low his life became before he kicked drink and my mother announced that she was getting the lawyers to cut Kitten's money off if she didn't sort her head out and then Mrs Minsk got very upset and shouted at my mother, 'She a little girl Mrs M-J! She not always like this. She in a mess! We all get mess sometime in life! But we get better again! Kitten needs stability in her life. We all can pull together in house and give her firm foundation to get better!' According to Knute it was all very emotional.

I'm not sure what Mrs M meant by the firm foundation bit. It's not like Kitten hasn't got money and a house to stay in and everything. What else does she need?

I do agree that Kitten wasn't always like this. She used to be really amazing. Like the best big sister ever. She was my big sister Kit-Kat with the neck splodge who would paint my face like a tiger and read me *The Very Hungry Caterpillar* two hundred times in a row and let me get all excited about the caterpillar turning into a butterfly every single time. We used to take Mother's old clothes and play dressing up and dancing shows all summer long and she'd tell me about the boys she fancied and teach me silly songs with rude words to annoy the au pairs. And when I woke up in the middle of the night with a bad nightmare and realized that Mother wasn't there and they'd forgotten to book a night-time nanny I would wander through and sleep in her bed cuddled into her back. She was always really warm and smelled of soap.

'Right, so basically you're saying,' I shouted at Mother as she searched for her house keys and called to Voychek outside that she was about to come out, 'no emails, no phone calls, no messages to reception, no visitors, no nothing at all. We should all just ignore Kitten until she is better?'

'Yes, Poppet,' my mother said, sounding exasperated. 'THOSE ARE THE RULES!'

'Fine!' I said, as Mummy left, slamming the front door behind her.

And yes, fair enough, I understand the rules now, but the thing is these days Poppet Zanzibar Montague-Jones increasingly believes that rules are there to be broken. I'm not turning my back on my big sister. I'm going to visit her at Paradise Vision as soon as possible.

TUESDAY 6TH OCTOBER

Even though I'm totally losing faith that therapy is the answer to the Montague-Jones family dilemmas, I've taken some nuggets of wisdom from things Dr Sarzberg has said to me. Even if, as Flash says, 'he just makes them up as he goes along'. Or even if, as Flash also says, his qualifications are from a made-up country and he's just swizzling large amounts of cash from the Montague-Jones family by telling them they need special one-on-one counselling which he charges two hundred quid for sixty minutes of, then he asks you to stop speaking after forty-five minutes and spends the final fifteen minutes working out when he can fit you in again. Flash says Dr Sarzberg is basically a criminal and we all laughed at him when he said that but we were laughing less when the police turned up at Dr Sarzberg's office last week to investigate him due to an 'anonymous tip-off'.

I asked Flash that morning if he knew anything about this and he looked up from his strawberry milkshake and paused Newsround on CBBC and said slowly with a totally straight face, 'I have absolutely no idea what you're talking about.'

But despite all of this, I think Dr Sarzberg made a good point the other day when he said, 'Poppet, you need to have more confidence in your own opinions. You come from a large, highly confident family, who always speak their minds and somehow your voice has been drowned out. You need to follow your instincts and your heart.'

I think this makes perfect sense.

I don't have any ruddy confidence in myself. I think I'm a bit of an idiot actually. I've always been a source of amusement to my family. When I was much younger, if I even picked up a tennis ball and threw it in the garden, Knute and Poppet would roll about laughing at how wonky my aim was, then they'd make me do it again and again and try my best to hit buckets and plant pots just so they could laugh until they were sick. And I used to feel totally humiliated and my face would go red. But these days I think, what's so amazing about being able to throw a ball?

When I was ten and I asked Mother where babies came from she told me that if you want to have a baby you have to lie in bed side-by-side with a man wearing pyjamas and hold hands tightly and wish for one and then it arrives on the doorstep and I TOTALLY BELIEVED HER and told everyone I could think of who would listen – Knute, Granny, Father – and they were all laughing at me and they still bring it up now.

'Ooh you're not going to be changing into your pyjamas over at Felix's?' Kitten always says. 'You know what happens when you hold hands in pyjamas! Babies!'

Sometimes I wish all the things people thought about me in the past could be left behind for good.

Of course, this would mean I'd have to stop teasing

Felix about that time our family and his family hired a huge house for the summer on the Isle of Wight together when Felix and I were both six. Felix piddled his pants on the hovercraft and Mrs Minsk had to handwash them in the ladies toilet and dry them with the hand drier. And fair enough, this was nearly ten years ago but it still makes me crack-up. Felix doesn't mind this story though. He laughs about it too. Felix isn't a stresshead like I am. Felix couldn't give a damn what anyone thinks about him.

Anyway, I had confidence in my own decisions today and did something pretty amazing. I went to Stanmore to Paradise Vision to visit Kitten.

And OK, it didn't go entirely as I'd envisioned it but it wasn't wholly a fiasco either. I mean, there wasn't the part I was hoping for when Kitten ran sobbing down the corridor and scooped me up in her arms smothering me with kisses telling me how she's remembered all over again what an amazing little sister I am. That did NOT happen. But I'm still glad that I went. I learned a lot of things today that will be really useful when I leave Octavia Square behind and live my own life, which I'm increasingly certain that I will do.

I left school at 3.30pm as usual this afternoon, but I'd been rather sneaky and made Matthew cancel the car scheduled to take me home. I lied to Matthew, saying I needed to stay at least four hours later at the Lycée to do extra sculpting, as I was at a crucial point of chiselling the willy on my marble Roman centaur which Mother is determined will be the starring exhibit in the Young Sculpting Talent Preview at the ICA gallery next month. My mother is obsessed with this sculpting exibition and has set about bribing everyone involved in the exhibition to make sure my work is accepted.

I feel a bit guilty about this to be honest. It's suddenly started to dawn on me that when Mother does this sort of thing, then some other random girl who actually CAN sculpt is losing her place just because her mother can't afford to offer the judges a lovely free two-week holiday in Mustique. Meanwhile I'm going to end up with one of the best gallery spaces in Britain showing what is basically the misguided crashings and smashings of a talentless fifteen-year-old who has basically attacked a piece of marble with a chisel for ten weeks with all the finesse of a visually impaired, mid-seizure epileptic! I feel a bit bad about that actually. But I suppose that's just what life is like isn't it? Rich people have always got to do the most exciting stuff. I suppose that's just the way life is.

'If it's OK,' I said to Matthew, 'I'll call you later and tell you when I want to go home.'

'No problem, sweet pea,' said Matthew. 'You have a nice sculpting session. Give that marble HELL.'

I hung up and wondered how the heck I'd get to Stanmore without a chauffeur. I certainly couldn't risk taking one of Mother's cars to Paradise Vision as all the drivers aside from Cyril are complete bloody telltales and

LOVE grassing me up for things as Mother is known to hand out fifty-pound tips.

Last term, when Striker and I were sharing a Marlboro Light round the side of the school one evening after French tuition, we were spotted by Voychek, my mother's Polish driver, and my mother knew about that ruddy cigarette before we'd even managed to stub the thing out. I don't even smoke. I only had three draws on it as Striker was egging me on, but Voychek saw one of them and basically sold me down the river for fifty pounds. I hate Voychek now. He's enormous and he smells of bad aftershave and he's got big sticky-out ears and he used to work for the Polish military and he thinks he still does.

I thought about all this for ages in Maths today and began to realize I was going to have to take that public transport thing people are always discussing whenever Dad listens to Radio 4. My stomach was churning just contemplating it.

I borrowed Lady Iris's MacBook Air and tried to find out about timetables and stuff. It seemed the best way to Stanmore was to find one of those bus stop thingamejigs on the side of the road and find a bus going from Hampstead to Kilburn, then try to catch one of those underground tube things to Stanmore, then work it out from there.

The more the day went on, the more petrified I became. I've never been anywhere like this on my own before ever. I kept remembering a debate we had in class about public transport when the Mayor of London announced he was spending millions and millions of tax payers' money on hundreds of new buses. Well Blitzen was getting all het up, calling the bus the 'peasant wagon' and saying she'd rather die than set foot on one. Blitzen said this is why her father keeps loads of his money offshore in foreign accounts so he doesn't have to pay for stupid schemes for poor people like this. Blitzen said that if you're at the stage of life where you can't afford your own car then you're obviously screwed and you may as well kill yourself. Blitzen said that's what she would do if she had no money. She'd just kill herself straight away. Blitzen said just the thought of being locked in a metal box on wheels with random scumbags all coughing up their diseases onto her brought her out in a rash.

Then Amelia said that she had to get on a bus once in Mill Hill East, due to her mother's assistant making a massive balls-up of coordinating her pick-up from ballet lessons and she's never been so scared in her life. Amelia said she was sure she was going to get stabbed so she stood right at the front with the driver and pleaded with him to keep an eye on her. Then everyone in my class agreed that I DEFINITELY shouldn't go on public transport at all and neither should Lady Iris as we're related to the Royal Family so we'd probably get kidnapped by Muslims and have our heads cut off and the video would be shown on Al Jazeera TV. I worried about this all day today then I decided that if I wanted to see Kitten then I'd have to take this risk.

When the end-of-day bell rang, I slipped out of the front gates with all the other Hampstead Lycée girls and walked to the end of the road and then turned left and ran quickly away from the school, vaguely in the direction of Kilburn. I'd brought one of Knute's travel compasses with me and a water bottle and some chocolate incase I felt faint from hunger, and I knew I needed to be headed North. I kept checking the compass in my pocket and I seemed to be heading in the right direction, which I've got to admit was giving me quite a buzz.

Eventually I spotted one of those bus stop thingies. I walked up and stood by it and stared for a while trying to work out what it does. Did I need to call anyone and tell them I was here? It wasn't exactly clear. The sign on the pole said 'Towards Kilburn' and underneath was an electric noticeboard with flashing red letters that said:

Kilburn 138 – 8m
Kilburn 47 – 12m

How it could possibly be 1388 miles to Kilburn on the bus? How? It couldn't be that far away could it? Maybe it meant 1388 metres? How far was 1338 metres? And why was the bus underneath that 4712 metres? Or miles? Wasn't Africa three thousand miles away? I felt like giving up and going home.

Then suddenly a little old lady with a shopping trolley tutted loudly and said, 'Eight minutes for a 138 to Kilburn! What a liberty! I've been waiting here half an hour.'

Oh Lordy! I suddenly realized the sign meant that the 138 bus to Kilburn was coming in eight minutes! Except now it was saying seven minutes!

'Erm, pardon me,' I said to the lady. 'How long do you estimate it will take me to to travel to Kilburn please?'

'Eh?' said the lady.

'I'm wondering how long the journey will take? Is it lengthy?' I said.

The woman stared at me and thought about what I'd said. 'Len-thy? What you sayin'?' she said. She seemed stumped. Then suddenly her face lit up and she said, 'Oh, how far? I see! Oh, ten minutes, dear. Kilburn is just down the road!'

'Super!' I said, feeling a bit giddy. The woman laughed then like I'd told her a joke. The bus arrived and I started to feel nervous again. The old woman stepped forward and put her hand out, so I copied her but I felt terrified as it pulled up closer as it was enormous and noisy and could easily squash you dead, then a gust of wind nearly blew up my school skirt. The old lady stepped on and sort of waved her hand at the driver then sat down, so I walked up behind her and said to the driver who was sitting in the glass box, 'Hello! I'd like to go to Kilburn please! But can you tell me where to get off as I don't know where it is thank you.'

The driver sort of jumped like he was totally not expecting me to talk to him. 'You got Oyster?' he said.

'Pardon?'

'Show me your Oyster,' he said, looking terribly bored.

'Oyster?' I squeaked. It sounded like something bleak that Marmaduke Adams would ask while pointing at your groin area and offering you a packet of peanut M&Ms as a bargaining tool. I have since found out that an Oyster card is a pre-paid travel card that Londoners who are forced to do this public transport thing all the time carry with them. It does not mean your hairymary. Thank God.

'Yes, Oyster card!' the driver repeated quite slowly. He was getting a bit impatient.

'Er, I've got a Coutts credit card,' I said, getting my wallet out. 'Can I pay with that?'

The driver rolled his eyes at me.

'You got no Oyster?' he said. 'One pound fifty then.'

'Right, where do I put the credit card?' I said. 'Where do I type the PIN number?'

'Not your credit card! Your money! I need one-fifty in cash,' he said, with a sigh.

This was going very, very badly.

Then someone halfway down the bus shouted, 'Oh, for God's sake can we get a move on!'

'But I don't have any actual, like, money!' I said.

This was true. I never carry money. Neither does Mother and neither does Granny and neither does the Queen. Everything in my life like my school lunch or school trips is billed to my mother. And if Vixen and Striker and I go out for dinner we just use credit cards. Why would anyone go around with actual money? It's smelly and dirty and the coins are really heavy and it makes your pockets lumpy!

'I'm terribly sorry, I've not got any cash,' I said again.

'Oh, bloody hell, love, just sit down.' The driver sighed again loudly and pointed me down the bus. I ran past and found a seat and the bus set off slowly down the road.

I was trying to stay calm but my head was beginning to spin out. What if I got totally lost and missed my stop. I could end up anywhere. I could end up in the Cottingham Estate and my family would probably never see me again. In fact Blitzen was saying in class the other say that there are African families in the Cottingham Estate who practise Voodoo and sacrifice LIVING CHILDREN, so we all have to be extra careful letting our little brothers and sisters play on Hampstead Heath as they might get snatched.

So I was freaking out about this, and then, to make matters MUCH WORSE, a big fat man with man boobs got on to the bus and did the hand wavy thing at the driver then saw the space beside me and his big moon face sort of lit up and he plonked his big wobbly bum cheeks on the seat and almost sat on my thigh! Then he put an iPod on his ears, reached into his plastic shopping bag, unwrapped a cold meat pie and started pushing it into his face, making a sound like 'CHAM-CHAM-CHAM-CHAM-SLURPPPPPPP!!'

So now, as well as worrying about missing my stop I was TRAPPED behind a mountain of man boobs, blubber and pastry crumbs. For the first time in my journey I could feel tears coming to my eyes, but I pinched my hand and told myself to get a bloody grip of my head and be fierce like Striker Earhart would be in this situation. In fact I was thinking, 'Why the hell didn't I bring Striker? I can't do this alone!'

Just as all this started to get the better of me I spotted something amazing: a red sign with 'London Underground' on it! It was Kilburn Underground Station! I'd made it there alive!

I jumped up and squashed past the fat man which meant brushing my face against his cleavage – GROSS!!! – then I realized the bus was actually quite fast and was maybe not going to stop. So I looked around at all the other passengers and I yelled, 'I WANT TO GET OFF!!!'

There was a silence and everyone pretended I was invisible for a second and then someone said, 'Well ring the bleeding bell then!'

'What bell!' I yelled.

'Here!' said a boy in a tracksuit. He got up and he put his finger out about twenty centimetres and touched a black button on the back of a seat. There was a loud bleeping sound and a sign started flashing which said: 'BUS STOPPING'.

How the hell are you supposed to know how to do all of this sort of stuff?

I ran down the steps into Kilburn Underground station. It was really really scarily busy down there. I've never been anywhere as full of people before. There were hundreds and hundreds of people everywhere jostling into me and knocking me and asking me to move out of the way, including a group of those feral hoodie kids Mummy always warns me about, nudging each other, laughing about my school uniform which I was seriously wishing I'd not kept on.

I stood by the barriers for ages staring at the ticket machines totally confused by the hundreds of different types of tickets and the tube map which looked like a bowl of Mrs Minks's spaghetti bolognese thrown on to the floor.

Then a man in a navy blue jacket and trousers walked right up to me and said, 'Need any help, love?'

'And you are?' I asked, possibly a little bit rudely, but I was worried he was a confidence trickster trying to steal my Coutts card.

'Calm down, sweetheart, I work for London Underground,' he said. He had a name badge on that said 'Bob'.

I stared at him and opened my mouth and shut it

again. Would a thief or a pervert go to the trouble of making a badge that said 'Bob'? I didn't know.

'Where do you need to be?' he said, 'There's a good service tonight on all lines.'

'Stanmore,' I said, holding my school bag tight to my body.

'Coming back today?' he said.

'God, yes,' I said.

'You need a Zone 1 to 6 travelcard then. That's your cheapest bet.'

I must have looked at him really pathetically then, because he said, 'Oh come on I'll show you! And took me to the machines, helped me buy a ticket, then walked me back to the barriers saying, 'Platform six, they go every five minutes at the moment. Have a nice journey!'

I couldn't believe anyone could be so kind and lovely without wanting something in return.

An escalator took me down to what seemed like the centre of the earth. Like REALLY, REALLY FAR DOWN, then I jumped on to a tube train which I can't remember anything about as I had to use some of Knute's transcendental meditation trances to zone out the horrible panicky feeling that I was literally underneath the earth's surface and any minute the soil could come crashing in and suffocate us all.

When the announcer finally said, 'This is Stanmore. All change please! Please mind the gap!' I ran out of the tube carriage, then up the escalator two steps at a time, out of the barriers and up to the fresh air on the main road where I stood puffing and panting.

A black taxi was sitting on the kerb beside the station and so I ran towards it and said, 'Do you take credit cards!? I need to go to Paradise Vision Rehabilitation Centre please? Do you know where that is?'

'Oh yeah, darling,' the driver laughed. 'Everyone knows where that is.'

I jumped in the car and we travelled down several long roads and then into what felt like the countryside, then down a long lane where I saw a big house. It looked a bit like an old vicarage that mother once hired us for the summer in Cornwall when we were a little. A big shabby-looking place with black iron gates and a gravel drive.

'Here you are,' said the cab driver. I paid him and got out. As I walked up, a couple of women in dressing-gowns poked out from the side of the building and then ran off giggling. I looked through the front windows and I could see two people playing ping-pong and in another room a man and a woman were sitting on chairs facing each other, a bit like I do when I have to chat to Dr Sarzberg.

I walked through the main doors into reception and I was rather shocked. The place was really quite sordid. It was dusty and depressing and smelled like disinfectant and the wallpaper was sludge coloured and the carpets were worn and stained. It wasn't like I imagined it would be at all. I thought it would be like a really amazing boutique hotel, all white and full of flowers and amazing furniture, like somewhere my mother might have interior designed.

A really tough-looking blonde woman standing behind a desk looked up at me and said, 'Yes?' But before I could say anything a man, who was about thirty, dressed in a grubby tracksuit, who looked totally ill like he was dying, appeared and started arguing with her about 'his medication', saying he wanted it now and she was 'a bitch' for not giving him it and he was signing himself out immediately.

The woman turned round and said in a rather angry voice, 'Daniel, we can only give you your meds when there's three of us to watch you take them, because that's the rule ever since you started *not* taking them and selling them to other patients! Now go back to the day room as I am very busy!' The man sloped off. She turned back to me then.

'Yes!'

'I'm here to see my sister Kitten Montague-Jones, please!' I said.

The woman looked at me suspiciously.

'Kitten isn't receiving any visitors. It's on her records. Her family have requested it. And I'll tell you now, if you're a reporter trying to pull a fast one, I will call the police now and prosecute you for trespassing.'

'I'm not a reporter!' I said. 'I'm her sister! I'm Poppet Montague-Jones! Look!' I got my Coutts card out and showed her. Then I saw a crumpled copy of *Heat* magazine behind the desk and I said, 'Hang on, I think I can prove it even more! Pass me that!'

So she gave me the mag and I opened it up and there was me and Kitten on page 37 in the Stars Out Shopping section. It was a day two months ago, when me and Kitten called a truce and went shopping for a birthday gift for Mrs Minsk together. A creepy paparazzi guy followed us all afternoon long and took about five hundred different photos of us, right up close in our faces about a metre away, until Kitten eventually snapped and told him he was freaking us out and to bugger off please, so the magazine printed that one as part of their Stars Going Crazy! section too.

'That's me standing with Kitten, there!' I said.

The woman looked at it.

'Hmmn. OK,' she said. 'Why are you here? I thought the decision was not to visit.'

'We've changed our minds,' I said. 'Can I just say hello for five minutes, please?'

The woman sighed, then she picked up the phone, made a call and then told me to sit down. So I sat there waiting for my big reunion with my sister with the kissing and the hugs, but it didn't really come. Instead, a door swung open and suddenly stood in front of me was a rather rattled-looking Kitten, wearing trackpants, a man's T-shirt and no makeup. Her hair was all wavy like she'd washed it but had no straighteners or hair spray. She looked different to the last time I saw her. She was cleaner, less tired-looking, but definitely angrier than ever before.

'What the bloody hell are you doing here!?' she shouted. 'You're the bloody reason I'm in here, you little brat!'

I stayed sat down. I thought if I was seated there would be less chance of me picking up a chair and hitting her with it.

'I'm here to say hello,' I said calmly.

'OH HELLO!' she said, waving sarcastically. 'Do you know what those bastards have done to me? Do you? I have to stay here for twenty-eight days without a drink or a drug or a pill of any description and I'm not even allowed to have caffeine! And if I don't make it to twenty-eight days those idiots known as our parents are disinheriting me and having a block put on my bloody trust fund due to diminished responsibility!'

'How is this my fault!' I said, losing my temper slightly. 'You're the bloody drug addict, you silly cow!'

'Because you dobbed me in, you little turd!' she shouted. 'They didn't know I was taking drugs!'

'Oh, Kitten, don't make me laugh. *Everyone* knows you're taking drugs. People in Australia know you're a drug addict. And anyway, you've been here about bloody ten days, you've not got that long to go! Suck it up, you wimp!'

'I've got twenty-eight days to go!' Kitten screamed back at me.

'How?' I said.

'Kitten returned to Day One of the programme this morning,' said the receptionist. 'She was caught buying Diazepam off Daniel that was just in here.'

'THEY'RE ONLY BLOODY DIAZEPAM!' screamed Kitten. 'My mother takes Diazepam for her back. We take them on flights to knock ourselves out!'

'They're a controlled substance which should not be taken without a doctor's supervision!' said the woman firmly.

I sat very quietly and said nothing. Everyone in our family takes Diazepam. I didn't know that was illegal.

Kitten glared at me and said, 'Well I hope you're happy, Poppet!'

I closed my eyes and sighed slowly. 'I am glad actually, Kitten,' I said. 'I'm glad you're getting some help. And I'm glad I came to see you. I miss you.' Kitten's face sort of flickered for a second when I said that, like I'd said something that touched her. Then she turned on her heel and shouted, 'Well you'll just have to keep on missing me because I'll be here for bloody ever. Don't visit me ever again! Piss off!'

Then my big sister stormed off back into the clinic and slammed the door.

I left Paradise Vision soon after and made my way back to the Hampstead Lycée. The journey home wasn't as bad as the way there. I was quite calm really. I knew more what I was doing this time. And now I've written it all down, it sounds like I've had a terrible day, but I totally haven't, I've had a wonderful day really. I've learned to use public transport and I did it all on my own. I can go literally ANYWHERE. My life will never be the same ever again. And I've worked out how to get to my sister and help her get better.

I'm going to visit Kitten again as soon as possible. I'm not giving her any choice about it.

SATURDAY 10TH OCTOBER

I went on another Kitten expedition today.

I've left it six days before I dare chance the whole adventure again. I needed to let the fuss die down after last time, because when the nurse rang my mother to inform her that Kitten had been kicked back to Day One of rehab, she also informed her that 'Kitten's younger sister' had visited the secure wing too.

Secure wing?!! Ha ha ha! I walked straight in! And today when I turned up, the gates were standing open and the front door was on the latch and I just walked in with another family who were signing in to see their son, then I went to the visitors' room. Nobody stopped me at all. This place costs twenty grand per week! That's why it's full of the richest people in the world's kids, all sitting about in dressing-gowns trying to get clean of drugs and drink.

I wonder what happens if you're poor and you

become a drug addict? I suppose you just lie in the street until you die of it. A bit like that man I saw sitting beside the cash machine in Kilburn last week, covered in grime, holding a plastic cup, begging for coins. He didn't look that much different to how Kitten or her friend Daniel with the Diazepam from Paradise Vision looked.

But the man by the cash machine musn't have a mother who can afford to send him to rehab. That doesn't seem very fair at all really does it? I keep thinking about how life isn't fair at the moment and it's making me kind of sad. I keep trying to remember that thing Granny always tells us about how the Montague family should never feel guilty about how much money we have because much of our wealth is down to us being part of the British royal family for centuries, and the royal family are chosen by God. Granny says this is how God wants the world order to be organized and if we were to let guilt take over and influence us to give away all our power and wealth to the poor then we'd be basically totally annoying to God.

I don't even know if I believe in God. And if he does exist why would God want my family to be rich and other people to be poor? And if I'm starting to wish the world was fairer, does that mean I should ring up the Queen and say I want to give up my place in line to the throne? Oh Lord, I do hope not, as to be honest being eighty-seventh in line to the British throne is the main reason Blitzen Trapper lets me breathe the same air as her at school.

So anyway, when my mother got the call from the Paradise Vision clinic she took it extremely badly. She sort of went into one of those rapid-advance mental meltdowns she very often suffers and she threw her Blackberry halfway across the living-room, chased me up the stairs into my bedroom, then got right up in my face, so close I could literally smell the blackened cod she'd just eaten at Nobu for lunch.

'DID YOU VISIT KITTEN?!' she squawked. 'After everything I *expressly* said? How could you do that, Poppet? How?'

Mother seemed sort of furious. So furious, in fact, that I had to call upon a skill I've learned recently which is proving incredibly handy. I told an amazing whopping lie.

'Of course I didn't visit Kitten!' I said, pulling a wounded expression, as if the mere accusation would mentally scar me for ever. 'What an ABSURD thing to say! How would I get to Stanmore? It's about eighty miles away isn't it? Did I take Daddy's private jet or something?'

Mother stopped when I said that. Her face seemed to calm down a little. Obviously in reality I know Stanmore is about ten miles away, but the fortunate thing about being the Montague-Jones family dunce is you can play the idiot a lot of the time and it's totally believable.

'Well, apparently,' said Mother, 'a young woman

visited the clinic a few days ago and asked to see her *sister*. And Kitten agreed, but then changed her mind and stormed off after about two minutes.'

My mother and I were standing face to face. I kept my expression totally calm, just like Daddy taught me to do when I play poker. I needed to see if there was any more incriminating information. Did the nurse give a description of me or anything? It seemed not.

'It was probably a journalist, Mother,' I sighed. 'All the newspapers are DYING for an exclusive picture of Kitten in rehab looking all "boo-hoo me" without her makeup bag aren't they!? Bettina in my class says that *Star!* magazine is bloody TEDIOUS and DULL ever since you sent Kitten away. Bettina says the pages are just full of ruddy boring, healthy, vegan celebrities going to film premieres and talking about yoga and their new acting projects. Bettina says no one wants to read about that! Bettina says life is tonnes duller now that there's no pictures of Kitten drunk out of her mind doing forward rolls down the red carpet, or getting arrested outside the Ritz for trying to steal one of the antique lamps in the restaurant or, like, punching a paparazzi guy on our front doorstep.'

I stopped talking and realized to my amazement that my mother was actually listening to me. This was a momentous, experience. In fact it was rather freaking me out.

'So,' said Mother. 'You think *journalists* might be trying

to get into the building to see her?'

'Well it wasn't me was it?' I said, fake-laughing. 'Hey, unless I got one of those bus things there, eh? Imagine that? Ha ha! Ooh hello, I'm Poppet! I'd like to get on the bus please! Yeah right!' I did a little mime of me trying to get on the bus and not being able to find the door.

My mother's face broke into a little smile imagining such a ludicrous idea.

'OK, OK,' she said. 'And I suppose you caught an underground train too, did you?' Mother looked ashamed now for accusing me.

'Ha ha, yes!' I said. 'I went on a tubeytrain, or whatever it's called! Ha ha!'

'Oh, Poppet, just imagine?' she said. 'Imagine either of us down there "on the tube" totally trapped amongst the great sweating unwashed rabble?! It's unthinkable isn't it! Imagine how filthy our clothes would be by the time we came out! I'd have one of my panic attacks, I know I would!'

'Oh SHUT-UP! Don't!' I smiled. 'You're making me feel faint. Let's not even imagine, Mummy!'

'OK, darling,' she said squeezing my arm. 'Sorry for making a fuss. I'm sure you're right. It must have been a reporter. Look I've really not got time to worry about this whole Kitten thing today as I'm at a crucial point with a project I'm working on. Wish me luck now, I'm off for a mega-important chat with my lawyers.'

'Good luck, Mummy,' I said. She leaned forward and

kissed me on the forehead and wandered off. As she closed the door to my room, I hopped off the side of my desk where I'd been perched while we talked. Underneath my bum cheeks sat the shiny new turquoise Oyster card which I'd bought on my way home last week, pre-charged with one hundred pounds' worth of credit. It was so easy to buy I couldn't believe it. It took about one minute! I don't know if I'll ever in my entire life use up that much money on public transport, but the thought that I could at any time just get on a bus or a tube and ride away and be somewhere else makes me very very giddy indeed. And today's journey to Stanmore was a LOT smoother than last week's. This time I dressed down in jeans and a T-shirt and trainers and remembered to leave behind the diamond ring I always wear on my left-hand index finger which I've worked out now is a bit flashy to wear around normal folk. Granny gave me the ring as a twelfth birthday present, it was one that the King of Monaco gave her when she was dating him a long time ago in the 1950s. It's my favourite thing ever and I feel bare without it, but I know Mr Chenowitz, the accountant keeps going bonkers at my mother for letting me even wear it at all, what with it being worth about half a million, so I thought I best leave it in my bedroom.

At about 9am this morning I packed a small bag with presents for Kitten and slipped out of the house. I told Mrs Minsk I was off to a spinning class with Vixen, then we were studying all day at her house so I'd be late home, then I set off walking very quickly from Octavia Square ducking and diving down sidestreets and back lanes I've never even seen before trying to stay off main roads where I could be spotted by some nosy mother or a member of our staff looking to make a quick lump sum of cash.

I needed to find a bus stop in any of the streets in Hampstead that went vaguely in the direction of Kilburn. The first bus that seemed vaguely right went a really, really long route around about twenty roads to places I'd never heard of, but I knew the quicker I got out of sight the better.

The 671W bus was terribly busy when I got on and as it trundled along it got fuller and fuller until the whole aisle was blocked with people standing up and everyone seemed to have at least one baby and three bags of shopping on their knee and everyone was talking to each other or chatting on mobiles or listening to their iPods loudly. It was very noisy indeed!

Then after about ten minutes I looked around and realized something very, very weird indeed. I was the only person with white skin on the bus! Everyone else had either dark brown skin, light brown skin, or maybe they were just really tan coloured like they were from Latin America. There was also a few Chinese or Japanese people and some ladies whose skin I couldn't see at all as it was totally covered up with just a slit in the fabric to see their eyes. Then there was me. A little white girl with sort of porridge-coloured skin.

This felt bizarre. Like totally the opposite of how life normally is, isn't it? I mean, obviously, I do know some non-white people. In fact I know two of them, like my friend Alitash whose father is the Ethiopian Ambassador in London, she is lovely. And I know Indira whose family are from Bombay in India and she is a complete sweetheart. In fact when Indira's daddy, who is Chairman of the Bank of India, threw that amazing ball at the Dorchester Hotel with all the dancing and two real life baby elephants that you could feed apples to, well, there was a lot of people wearing saris and turbans and stuff and it was jolly good fun.

But this whole 'being the only white person' thing was a new thing for me. I suddenly thought, Gosh this must be what Indira and Alitash feel like every day. Like, ALL THE TIME!

Then a Muslim lady in a headscarf and a blue dress got on holding a baby in her arms and pushing another baby in a pram and she seemed to be in a fluster trying to get everything sorted as the bus set off again, so I jumped up and helped her hold the baby while she balanced bags on the back of the pram.

'Thank you very much, you're very kind,' she said. Then we both sat down and I played peek-a-boo with the baby until he was giggling like crazy and at this point I was thinking why don't me and Vixen and Striker just get on the bus and go places a lot more? I looked out of the window and noticed we were parked beside three enormous apartment blocks in a row and a small children's play park.

The apartments weren't pretty at all. Nothing like the nice ones down in Chelsea that my father bought one of last year as an investment. These apartments were sort of a browny-grey colour and the balconies had knickers and underpants drying on them, or barbecue sets, which was totally weird as they were hardly big enough for a person to even stand on. Some of the balconies had Union Jack flags hanging off them, even though it didn't seem at all like somewhere the Queen would visit, ever. Some apartments even had smashed windows or looked like they had been on fire at some point.

Beside the play park was a sort of hall or meeting centre. It had grafitti all over the doors and there were kids sitting outside on the steps smoking cigarettes, with those Staffordshire bull terrier dogs that are either illegal or should be made illegal as it's always in the news that they have like a genetic fault that makes them want to eat babies.

The whole place was ruddy depressing and rather terrifying to be honest. Indeed, I felt a bit scared again now. And to make matters worse lots of people got off here and loads of new people got on, including about five rough-looking, hard girls who were about my age, wearing hoodies or little padded jackets with fur trimmed hoods and gold earrings and loads of makeup. Three of the girls were black and two were white and they had lip piercings and eyebrow piercings and that hair thing happening where it's sort of braided close to their head in patterns then the rest is up in bunches leaving some bits sticking up. They were wearing leggings with no socks and trainer boots with the laces undone and the tongues of their boots were all hanging out messily. One of the black girls had tattoos of blue flowers on her hands and one of the white girls had a bird on her neck and some firey flames coming out of her bum crack. I saw it when she bent over to take a little brown baby out of a pram.

'Oh my dayz, he looks well like his daddy,' one of the other girls said, pointing at the baby, and the girl who was the mother said, 'Yeah, whateva, my baby ain't even met his daddy, innit. His daddy is a wasteman, innit. I giving Tyrelle air until he gives me my cash, get me? He ain't bein no babydaddy until he fronts up with cash iznit?'

I listened to what she said and tried to replay it in my head. I was pretty sure it was English. I could sort of figure out 'babydaddy' but what was 'a wasteman'? I think maybe she might have got pregnant by one of the men who takes away their dustbins. Finally we pulled away from the bus stop and I finally noticed a sign by the side of the road which made me nearly poo my own pants. It said, 'COTTINGHAM ESTATE'.

My heart started thumping like crazy. I had made a REALLY REALLY bad mistake getting on this bus. One I could end up regretting for ever! I closed my eyes tightly and tried to get my breathing under control by imagining I was a leaf floating gently through the Peruvian Rainforests.

'OK, Poppet, BREATHE,' I told myself. 'You're FINE! OK, you've got yourself lost in the Cottingham Estate. Don't panic. At least you're now DRIVING AWAY IN THE OPPOSITE DIRECTION and you've got away with your life!'

I sat there shaking, thanking God, who I don't even believe in properly, for delivering me from the jaws of hell without any of these girls working out I was one of the 'snobby cows from Hampstead Lycée', then trying to chloroform me and steal my kidney to sell to someone who needs a transplant. Blitzen says this sort of thing happens A LOT in the Cottingham Estate. Blitzen says this is why you should NEVER drink an alcoholic drink anywhere in public except in the VVIP room of an exclusive club as you're bound to get drugged and abducted by chavs from the Cottingham and wake up in one of their rubbish skips, twenty-four hours later, with a missing lung, which is already in a box on its way to America.

However, as the bus continued slowly down the road and started drawing closer to Kilburn Underground Station, my head stopped spinning, my breathing returned to normal and I glanced around the bus at all the people chatting on their phones or reading newspapers and I started thinking maybe I'd been a bit silly. Basically I'd just travelled right through the Cottingham Estate on a BUS and nothing terrible had happened to me at all. Either lots of people I knew had been telling lies about the Cottingham, or I'd just been very very lucky. I couldn't work out which.

Today's meeting with Kitten was marginally better than the last week's one. Like, maybe ten per cent better. Twenty percent? OK, I can't do maths, but I do know that we had made PROGRESS. I mean, fine, OK, me and Kit weren't exactly like, hugging each other and making plans to go on a girlie spa retreat when she gets out, but we did manage to make it a full nine minutes before the extreme 'boo-hoo me' and stropping off stage started. And when I gave Kitten her gifts she didn't refuse to take them or throw them at my head or anything.

I took Kitten some of Mrs Minsk's homemade jam tarts that I know she used to love. We used to have them with milk when the au pair brought us home from school years ago. This was before Kitten got sent away to boarding school and ended up on a stupid diet as she was obsessed with staying under eight stone.

That's the only thing Kitten learned at boarding school, a really weird attitude to meals. She certainly didn't get any GCSEs.

Kitten opened the plastic box with the jam tarts inside, smelled them then closed it again. Then I passed her a copy of *Flowers in the Attic* by V.C. Andrews which we both read years and years ago when we went to Dubai with Mummy and we were trapped in the hotel suite for days as she was always working. I know Kitten loves that book and, on her more civil days, has said she would like to read it again if she ever has time. Well Kitten definitely has time now, because she has returned to Day One of rehab, again. This is the third time Kitten has done Day One now!

Apparently two days ago Kitten had been behaving quite well and saying all the right things in therapy so she'd earned the privilege of having access to her hair straighteners. Except Kitten didn't use them to straighten her hair, she swapped them with a girl called Florence for three miniature bottles of Stolichnaya vodka.

I don't want to know where Florence had been hiding the Stolly vodka. I didn't ask. But Florence happened to be in Paradise Vision for chronic self-harming, so by 4pm there was a whole lot of screaming and Florence had been transferred to the local emergency department with second degree burns to her arms and legs and Kitten was in very serious trouble with the Paradise Vision management.

'I didn't know she was going to that did I, Poppet?' tutted Kitten. 'Bloody self-harming pleb! They were my limited edition, diamond encrusted GHDs too. The ones GHD themselves gave me when I modelled for them! Now that mental cow has left all her burned skin hanging off them!'

I sighed deeply when she said this.

'You do realize,' I said to Kitten, 'that the longer you keep on being a complete wanker, the longer you're going to be stuck here? You'll turn thirty in this place the way you're going. You'll spend your thirtieth birthday wearing a second-hand man's tracksuit playing ping-pong with heroin addicts in a big house that smells of, like, Flash's piddle.'

'Fine by me,' said Kitten, folding her arms.

So then I passed her the iPod Nano I'd brought her. She looked at me suspiciously for a moment then said, 'What's on this?' she said.

'It's a surprise,' I said.

Kitten tutted, 'It's not a message from the bloody family is it?' she said. 'As I DON'T WANT TO HEAR FROM THEM! In fact can you tell Mummy and Daddy that I HATE THEM and I don't need their STUPID INHERITANCE as I'm going to make my own way in this world and be a pop star or I'll write children's books or have my own fashion label or something and I'll be a billionaire anyway. TELL THEM THEY CAN SHOVE THEIR MONEY UP THEIR ARSES. Yes, tell them that!'

Kitten and I stared at each other in silence for a moment. 'Do you *really* want me to say that?' I said.

Kitten winced a bit then, 'OK, no,' she said sheepishly. 'Don't say that. OK, tell them I'm really, really unhappy here and they need to pull me out AS SOON AS POSSIBLE as I am considering killing myself and if I do die it will be totally their fault. And tell them I am banning you all from my funeral. In fact I'll write a letter for the vicar to read out that says, "JOCASTA AND JAMES MONATGUE-JONES, THIS IS ALL YOUR FAULT YOU TOTAL SELFISH KNOBHEADS!" And I'm going to make sure that they have big screens put up in Hyde Park so the overflow of mourners who can't get into St Paul's Cathedral can all hear my opinion about them FROM BEYOND THE GRAVE.'

Kitten sat back in her seat then and sort of gave a little smile as if she'd come up with a truly genius plan.

'Wow,' I said, as this last rant was sort of mental and self-absorbed, even by Kitten's standards.

'Well good luck killing yourself,' I said. 'As far as I can see they've taken away all your belts and shoelaces and ties and stockings and everything. And you have to eat your meals with one of those totally lame plastic fork/spoon things don't you? What are those things called again?' Kitten glared at me when I said that.

'A spork,' she said, through very small lips. I was clearly annoying her.

'Oh yes, that's it!' I said. 'A spork. Are you going to stab yourself to death with a spork? Gosh, that will take ages.'

'I haven't decided how I'll kill myself yet,' Kitten tutted, picking up the iPod and staring at it. 'Anyway, what's on this iPod if it's not a message.'

'I made you a playlist of happy songs.' I smiled. 'There's a bit of everything. I put the first Jack Penate album on. And that Fleetwood Mac album of Mother's that you like. Oh, and some new Scandinavian pop stuff that I stole off the internet this morning.' I put my hand out to take it back. 'I thought it might make you feel happy, but I can take it home if you want.'

'No, no don't do that,' she said, shoving it into her pocket. 'I'll keep it.'

We sat in silence for a while longer. Then she looked at the jam tarts in the box with 'Kitten' written in felt-tip on the lid and the tattered book which had been to Dubai and back and then she looked back up at me and said in a very quiet voice, 'Thank you.'

'It's fine,' I said quietly. 'I want you to come home, Kitten. I miss you.'

Kitten didn't say anything to that, she just looked down at the table.

'Do you think you'll be better soon?' I said.

Kitten tutted crossly. 'There's nothing wrong with me, Poppet!' she said, shaking her head like this whole thing was ridiculous. 'I mean, God, big wow, yeah I was taking cocaine. And a bit of Valium to sleep afterwards. And the odd ecstasy pill now and again. And, OK I was boozing quite a lot, like every day, but that's not, like, a lot by London standards is it? Everyone I know in my circle of friends was caning it much more than me! Why am I here? Why am I being made a scapegoat just because I'm the most famous?'

I didn't know what to say to this. The one thing I was trying to remember was something that Dr Sarzberg talked to me about recently, which is 'All feelings are valid'. Basically, this means that if someone is saying something right from their heart, then even if it's really really dumb and you don't agree with it, well it's still their opinion and that you should listen to it. All feelings are valid.

I like that idea. I tried to think about how Kitten felt.

'But Kitten,' I said. 'Just because some people are doing even more harm to themselves, it doesn't mean that we shouldn't worry about *you*. It doesn't mean that you're not a drug addict. It's *you* we're all worried about.'

Kitten scowled deeply.

'I'm not a drug addict!' she said, sounding like she was getting quite angry again. 'I just like having a good time! What's wrong with having a good time? What else do they expect me to do? Just sit in the house? Do you know what these counsellor idiots in here are saying to me, Poppet? They're saying that I should get through twenty-eight days of rehab, then lose contact with all of my old friends, stop going to Catastrophe 13, then begin a new life and work on getting myself physically and mentally fit. Like start JOGGING or MARTIAL ARTS! They say I should start enjoying simple things in life like seeing my family and watching a TV show, and not only should I never ever take drugs, I should never ever EVER have another drink of alcohol again. Never ever. CAN YOU IMAGINE THAT?'

I was trying to imagine it. I tried to envision our house without alcohol. I just couldn't. 1 Octavia Square without the bulging drinks cabinet? And the *Chateau Neuf du Pape* with supper, and the Bollinger champagne on Friday nights to celebrate the weekend starting, and the cocktail parties at Christmas, and Mummy and Daddy drinking vodka and tonics in the kitchen when Daddy flies in from New York, and Mummy's fabulous birthday parties in Tuscany where everyone gets totally wellied on booze and jumps in the pool.

No, I couldn't imagine it. For the first time ever, I felt a bit sorry for Kitten. It was like my parents were making her do something that really was impossible, something they couldn't even do themselves.

'But I'll help you!' I said. 'We'll find other things to do in London that don't involve any booze or any other of the bad stuff! There must be other things!'

Kitten looked at me disgustedly.

'We can . . . go and look at, like, museums!' I said. 'And we can bake cookies together like we did when we were little! And . . . and . . . we can plant some flowers in the garden! Hey remember when we planted the sunflowers, Kitten? And they grew so tall it started to freak us out? We could do that again! We could grow tomatoes and herbs . . . and potatoes!'

Kitten had stood up by now, she clearly wasn't in the

mood to listen to any more of my ramblings.

'Poppet, I'm not spending the rest of my life bloody stuck in Octavia Square growing potatoes with you, you annoying brat, I really would rather suffer death by spork.' Then she turned on her heel and huffed out of the visiting room.

Her parting comment didn't upset me at all to be honest. After some of the arguments and physical fights I've had with Kitten over the past few years, by her standards this was actually rather lovey-dovey. I was happy that I went.

I was in such a spirited mood when I left Paradise Vision that I decided to do something massively brave. I didn't get a bus straight back from Kilburn to Hampstead. I decided to get something to eat. I wanted to find one of those McDonald's places that Cyril took Flash and I to once. I wanted to buy one of those Mcflurrywurry thingies and maybe some French fries. Or maybe some soup or a slice of pizza or whatever McDonald's sell. I didn't have a clue what McDonald's sold to be honest and I didn't know whether I was supposed to call ahead and reserve a table or something, but I didn't care. I just made a snap decision and went for it. Poppet Montague-Jones is on FIRE right now!

Well, I have to say, the whole McDonald's experience was pretty crazy for more reasons than one. I got there at about 3pm which isn't anyone's official meal time as it's not lunch, dinner or supper, but the place was still very busy with six people queuing at every till.

I asked a man who was clearing up trays if there was a waiter service or even a VIP area with a more expensive menu but he just looked at me like I was saying, 'HELLO I AM JESUS CHRIST THE SAVIOUR LET ME ANOINT YOU WITH THE HOLY SPIRIT.'

'No, that's the queue,' he said, wandering off. I went and stood in one of the queues which seemed to be moving and stared at the menu on the wall behind the serving staff's heads. It didn't make any ruddy sense. They sold a thing called a Quarterpounder but I've no idea what it was a quarter pound of. Or how much a quarter pound weighed? They sold a thing called a Filet o' Fish, but it didn't specify what sort of fish or whether it was steamed or pan fried. Maybe it was like 'catch of the day' at Les Moules in Saint-Tropez and the head chef just serves you whatever is freshest? And what part of a chicken is the 'nuggets' exactly? Is that the breast meat? It was terribly confusing.

The rest of the menu appeared to be types of burgers but I didn't know whether I would like that at all as I've never really had one. Mother banned the au pairs from letting us eat any sort of burgers or sausage or mince years ago as she says it would give us Mad Cow Disease. Mother says that's what's up with all the feral kids in the Cottingham, they eat burgers all day and their brains are rotted away.

Suddenly, I was at the front of the queue, stammering,

sweating and trying to place my order.

'Can I have an, erm, burger please?' I said to a boy in a green visor and a T-shirt with stars on his name badge.

'Cheeseburger, Big Mac, Quarterpounder?' he said, poking a screen.

'What exactly *is* a Big Mac,' I asked.

'Eh?' said the boy.

'A Big Mac?' I said. 'What is it?'

I could see he had to think about this.

'It's, erm, well a burger,' he said. 'With like, another burger and some sauce and erm . . .' He looked totally stumped. 'IT'S JUST A BIG MAC. Like, a Big Mac. It's a burger.'

'OK, super,' I said, feeling pressure to make a choice, 'I'll have one of those then.'

'Wanna go large?' he said.

'Yes with goolarge, please,' I said. I didn't know what goolarge sauce was, but I decided not to ask any more questions as I could hear some girls behind me laughing, 'Oh and can I have a McFlurrywurry too.'

'Oreo, Smartie or Crunchie?'

'An ice cream one?' I said, and he shook his head a bit.

'Drink?' he asked.

'Oh, right, have you got like some guava juice or maybe a carbonated water with a pomegranate infusion?'

'We got Coke or Fanta,' he said.

'I'll have a Phantom,' I said. And then everyone

164

behind me laughed. My face started to go red. I realized my voice was standing out a mile and I needed to try and sound less like me. But I didn't know who else I could sound like.

'Five pound fourteen,' he said, starting to load up my tray with stuff.

'Oh, I'll need to use this,' I said, passing him my Coutts card. He took it and looked at it and his eyes widened.

'OK,' he said, then he put it in the machine covering it with his hand entirely so no one else could see it, as if he was trying to protect me or something.

I took my tray of Big Mac, goolarge and Mcflurrywurry and tried to find somewhere to sit, but the place was absolutely crazy. It felt more like being in a rowdy party than in a restaurant. People were squashed round tables, or standing up eating or shouting across at their friends and at one point one girl seemed to throw a milkshake at her friend. I looked round, wondering if the manager would throw them out, but I couldn't see anyone in charge.

Finally, I spotted a little table with one seat behind it, and I went and sat down.

I unwrapped my Big Mac and looked around to see if there was any knives and forks or sporks for me to eat it with, but everyone else was just eating with their fingers like they were at a picnic so I picked up the burger and stuffed it into my mouth and took my first bite.

It tasted OK. It wasn't very hot. It was sort of lukewarm. I chewed it a few times and at first it was salty then suddenly this HORRIBLE, HORRIBLE taste filled my mouth. I can only describe it as like, a salty, vinegary slimy caterpillar sneaking down my throat. OH MY GOD IT WAS VILE.

'Gngngngngn!' I groaned and opened up the burger to see what I'd just been poisoned with. Hiding inside was a weird green circle. It was a slice of some kind of alien life-form or something. 'YAK!' I said, and fished it out and wrapped it in a paper napkin, (although they don't seem to call the napkins 'napkins' in this McDonald's place, I asked the staff three times for a 'napkin' and they looked at me vacantly until I called it 'something to mop runny stuff up with.')

As I wrapped the poisonous object in a napkin, I suddenly heard someone giggling quite loudly. I looked up feeling a little cross by this point. The whole McDonald's experience was an utter circus, and I felt a bit like a clown I must say. I hadn't paid good money for disgusting food and to become a laughing stock.

'So you ain't feeling the whole gherkin thing then?' a boy's voice said. I was very irate I can tell you! I looked up at the boy, I looked into his eyes, and then I didn't say anything. Mostly because at that precise moment in time I absolutely couldn't think of a single word or phrase or sound to make at all. I honestly think, and this feels totally insane writing this, that he was the most beautiful boy I have ever seen in my entire life. In fact my stomach just went YAHAYAHYAYAYHAHAHAHAH! when I looked at him.

He had big, brown eyes and short, cropped black hair and amazing cheekbones. Even though he was sitting down behind a table I could tell he was at least six foot or so because he had wide shoulders and very long legs. His face was clever but a bit cheeky. His skin was brown, really dark brown, and his nose was a little bit wide and very cute. His forearms were toned and his teeth were white and the palms of his hands were a much lighter colour to the rest of him and he was just ruddy amazingly gorgeous. He was eating a burger too, but he had a science textbook out on the table as if he was revising or something.

'I just pick them out too,' he said, pointing at my napkin. His voice was sort of cockney London with a tiny, tiny bit of African like Cyril's, but not as strong. 'I don't know anyone who likes gherkins. They're rank.'

I opened my mouth and shut it again. He looked at me, probably believing me to be rather rude, then picked up his burger again and looked at his textbook.

'That was NEVER a gherkin?' I said. 'I am utterly bewildered by it! I'm taking it home to get a microscope on it!'

The boy looked at me and then he smiled. I'm sure he was smiling at my accent. Every time I open my mouth in the world outside of the Lycée and Octavia

Square people seem to either laugh at me or tut at me. I tried to think quickly of anything I could say that didn't make me sound like Granny or the Queen, but I just couldn't.

'Yes, it's a gherkin!' he said. 'I assure you.'

'But gherkins don't taste remotely like that,' I said. 'This is abysmal. I mean, when was it pickled? Gherkins are supposed to be a happy experience. An *amuse bouche* even, but this one is a wholly hateful experience. One out of ten I give it! No more today, thank you.'

The boy laughed at this. Like, really laughed like I'd said the funniest thing he'd ever heard.

'Have you never been to McDonald's before . . . erm . . .' he said. 'I didn't catch your name?'

'I didn't throw it,' I said, trying to be cool like Vixen would be.

'You gonna throw it, or what?' he said.

'Oh, I'm Poppet,' I said, wiping my hand and sticking it out. 'Enchanted to meet you! Yes, of course I've been to McDonald's. I'm here, like, all the time, I'm LOVING it,' I said pointing at the side of my Phantom drink which had this phrase written on the side.

'Poppet!' he said, 'I'm Kwame.' Then he put out his hand and I shook it.

His hand was warm, not sweaty at all, just warm and his handshake was strong. It felt like the world stood still. There was no way I would manage another mouthful of food, I felt like I was going to be sick, but happy sick.

168

'Cammy?!' I said, 'As in short for Cameron?'

'Kwame,' he said. 'KWAME.'

'Kwame?' I repeated.

'Kwame!' he said. 'It's quite common in London. It's African.'

'Are you from Africa?' I said.

'Erm, well yes,' he said. 'But no. I mean my great-grandmother was from Africa. I'm from just down the road. I was born in that hospital just over there. My mother called me Kwame as she likes to honour our roots in Ghana. Y'know instead of just giving us British names. She says it's important we remember the whole slavery thing. It's all good though. I'm fine with that. I like Kwame.'

'What whole slavery thing?' I said. He looked at me like I was joking and then he actually hooted with laughter.

'Slavery,' he said.

'Slavery?' I said. 'What does that mean?'

Kwame opened his mouth and shut it again, 'Slavery. The slave trade!' he said. 'That's like, how hundreds of thousands of Africans ended up in other places in the world!'

'What, they left Africa to get jobs in other countries?' I said.

'Erm . . . Yeah,' he said, he seemed a bit stumped. 'Sort of, a bit like that.'

There was a silence. I didn't know what I'd said wrong.

'Where are you from?' he asked me.

'Oh, I'm from, erm, just down the road too,' I said. 'My great-grandmother is from Britain though. I'm sort of totally British.'

I smiled at him when I said that. I was worried he was upset about this whole slavery thing which I was now beginning to worry was a very bad thing, but thankfully he didn't look cross, more intrigued. We both stared at each other then and there was a bit of a silence.

'What are you studying for?' I said, pointing at his book. 'I'm ruddy hopeless at science. I'll probably scrape a D in Biology and I even have two hours a week extra tuition too.'

Kwame's eyes widened when I said that, he looked really jealous.

'Oh my dayz!' he said. 'I'd love extra tuition. But it's well expensive. I've got to pass my Science GCSEs with As, you see? I want to be a doctor.'

I sat staring at him, saying nothing. I could imagine him doing this. He just had one of those faces like you'd trust him to get important things done.

'I want to specialize in fevers and viruses and hopefully go to Africa,' he said. 'Y'know a lot of the stuff they die from out there is quite simple to stamp out. They just need more drugs and medical help.'

'Gosh,' I said. 'That sounds terribly clever. I don't know what I'll do when I leave school. I mean I'll carry on into Year Twelve and Thirteen obviously, but then, maybe I'll do, like, a gap year or something.'

Kwame laughed. 'It's only a gap if you know what's happening at the end of the gap!' he said, teasing me a bit, but I didn't mind.

'Oh Lord, I haven't the foggiest,' I said, shaking my head. 'I still need to work that out. I mean I do a bit of sculpting but I'm not terribly good.'

'Sculpting?' Kwame said. There was a long pause. 'Like actually sculpting? Like with marble. Marble and a chisel. Like bang, bang, bang sculpting?'

'Yes, sculpting!' I said. My cheeks were feeling a bit hot again now.

'Like those rich artists do,' Kwame said. 'Then they sell them in galleries for millions?'

'Yes!' I said, what other type of sculpting was there?

'Hahahahhahahahahah!' he chuckled. 'You're a proper wind-up merchant,' he said. 'You're kidding aren't you?'

'Erm,' I said, realizing I'd said something really bad but there was a chance I could rectify it. 'Yes! Of course I am! I'm just kidding. Of course I don't do sculpting. That would be totally sad.'

Kwame laughed a lot then. He'd not eaten hardly any of his burger.

'I should call you Duchess,' he said. 'That's what you sound like. Y'know the Duchess of York? You know that Sarah one with the red hair. She was married to Prince Andrew?'

'Erm, yes,' I said, 'I think I've heard of her.'

I didn't want to tell Kwame that if you looked at Fergie's wedding photos my mother is on the back row in a flouncy peach dress. Mummy has known Sarah since she was little.

'You're like her,' he said. 'You're the Duchess.'

'Well that's fine by me,' I said, smiling. 'I'll just call you Kwame if that's OK.'

I was so happy at that moment, possibly happier than I've ever been in my whole life that I didn't see the terrible thing that was walking through the door. It was VOYCHEK, my mother's driver, standing by the tills ordering his dinner. BLOODY VOYCHECK!

'Oh my God,' I said. 'Kwame, I've got to go, I'll maybe see you again sometime? Here or something, right? Jolly nice to meet you!' I grabbed my bag and stood up.

'Hang on,' he said, 'did I say something wrong?'

'No, no, nothing, nothing,' I said, 'I've just remembered I need to be somewhere like half an hour ago. BYE!' Then I shot off out of the door and ran to find the bus stop. Luckily Voychek was too busy filling his fat face with burgers to notice me leave.

And now I'm back home in my bedroom I cannot stop thinking about Kwame. I can't get him out of my mind at all. I really hope I can see him again. I want to hear his amazing deep laugh and watch his long, brown eyelashes flicker as he talks. And I need to say sorry to him about all that 'not knowing about slavery' business. Because I've been on Wikipedia and read about what white people did to black people hundreds of years ago. Y'know, all that dragging them from their homes and off to countries against their will and working them until they died of exhaustion and EVEN WORSE STUFF too and it was really really jolly horrid.

In fact, the more I think about it, black people are incredibly ruddy patient and forgiving to even want to speak to white people at all. If it was the other way round I think we'd still be rather vexed.

SATURDAY 17TH OCTOBER

I thought I'd definitely get busted after my last trip to Paradise Vision, but I didn't.

Basically my mother has been so distracted recently I could have sliced my own head off with the gardener's scythe and replaced it with a cardboard box with a mouth roughly drawn on in lipstick and she'd possibly not have noticed. This is what Mother gets like when she's engrossed in a huge designing project. Mother says it has been a constant bind in her lifetime that 'when she's overcome by the urge to create, her view of the rest of the world is obscured by her artistic vision'.

I think this is a fancy way of saying 'I can't be arsed to think about anything else'. I think it's also why she's such a ruddy messy person and all of our cleaners eventually leave due to the continuous piles of her old tissues, half-full coffee cups and crumpled up pieces of paper and pairs of her pants she leaves in her trail as she rattles around our house like Hurricane Gloria.

I didn't even get the chance to ask Mother where she was flying off to this morning, but she has definitely gone. Her Louis Vuitton suitcase was in the hallway when I went to bed and had vanished by the time I got up. I do know Mother tried to stall her business trips as long as she possibly could, but Kitten's rehab is going on a lot longer than everyone imagined. The Chief Rehabilitation Supervisor called Mother yesterday and told her that there is basically no point in Kitten being in rehab if she's not 'committed to the programme' and she'd underlined this on Thursday by chucking a shoe at the forehead of a nurse who was trying to confiscate a strip of six Co-codamol painkillers Kitten had sellotaped to her inner thigh up quite close to her hairymary.

The Paradise Vision supervisor says that Kitten will continue to be a hopeless cause until her attitude becomes, 'more respectful and compliant'. I have to admit I nearly weed in my pants with laughter when I heard that.

Those are two words you'd never associate with my big sister. Kitten is like an angry bull let loose in Harvey Nichols' crystal glass department, even on her best days. Kitten never lets people tell her what to do and she has spent her whole life being disrespectful, being the loudest voice at any party and is generally only allowed back to someone's house a second time purely to apologize.

Kitten is actually very cool in a topsy-turvy way. It's funny how all the things that were aggravating me about Kitten are the things I miss so much now that she's not around. I just wish Kitten could take her special skills and use them for some good. Or am I being totally daft here?

When I got to Paradise Vision today, Kitten was sat in the garden looking in remarkably good spirits for someone who was in so much trouble yet again.

'Oh God, Poppet, it's no biggie,' she said, placing her hands under her skinny thighs on the garden bench. 'I mean Day One again. That's fine. I'm quite chilled out here. I've had some quite, y'know, decent chats with some of the counsellors recently. Some of them are actually almost human. And the knobhead I threw my shoe at is off with concussion and nervous stress now, so it's all worked out rather well.'

I stared at her and almost laughed but I stopped myself as this would be encouraging her.

'I thought Mummy and Daddy might have come and visited me by now,' Kitten said, a tiny bit sadly.

'Mmmm,' I said. 'Well they're doing tough love, remember.'

'Yeah,' she said. 'Well it's pretty damn tough, Poppet. I've been here like a million years.'

Obviously she was exaggerating but I got her point.

'Mummy flew away on business today,' I said. We

both paused then and watched as three nurses came storming out of the main building and cornered a young woman by the greenhouses, grabbed her arms, started feeling her boobs a bit, then suddenly one of the nurses said, 'Got them!' and held up a packet of twenty Marlboro Lights.

'Oh God, rookie mistake,' said Kitten. 'You're never going to keep anything hidden in your bra. That's the first place they look.'

We sat in silence for a while and then Kitten said, 'So where has Mummy gone to? New York?'

'I've no idea,' I said. 'I know all her projects have been really delayed since you've been here. She's been in a real state.'

'Well she can't be in that much of a state or she'd have come to see me!' Kitten said.

'I meant about her work,' I said.

'Oh,' Kitten said.

Kitten looked right and left and then behind her and then she reached down the front of her tracksuit bottoms, rustled about a bit and produced a rolled-up cigarette and a match. She struck the match on the bottom of the bench then lit the ciggie with it.

'Keep an eye out for me,' she said, then took a double draw. 'Y'know what Dr Sarzberg once said to me?' Kitten said. 'When I was in one of his one-on-one sessions with him?'

'No.' I said. 'Go on.'

'He said that sometimes it seemed like the Montague-Jones children were a crowd of people desperately trying to get the attention of their mother. That's why we all act mad.'

'Mmmm, yeah,' I said. 'He said something like that to me once too. He said that was maybe the reason I kept announcing I was going to kill myself, when I quite clearly wasn't.'

'Oh God, I do that too,' laughed Kitten. 'We all do that! Flash is always saying he'll kill himself. I thought all kids did that!'

'Apparently not,' I said. 'Apparently it's quite weird, y'know, all that dramatic flouncing off to one's bedroom every week waving a bottle of painkillers or a length of rope yelling GOODBYE CRUEL WORLD! Apparently that's just a Montague-Jones thing.'

'Crikey,' said Kitten. 'I never knew that.'

I felt a bit bad for Mummy then. It was like we were blaming her for everything. I was sure everything in the world couldn't be her fault. I love my mother very much. And deep down I know that Kitten does too.

'I think Mummy tries to do her best,' I said to Kitten. 'I think maybe the thing is that we all need to try a bit harder too. Maybe all the Montague-Jones family have to think about what's going wrong and try to meet in the middle. Maybe we need some new house rules?'

'I didn't think we had any house rules?' said Kitten.

'Maybe we need to get some house rules! Maybe that's the thing,' I said.

Then the bell rang to signal it was the end of visiting time. We both stood up and completely out of the blue we hugged each other. It was the first time Kitten and I have hugged for almost three years. My face got all pressed up against her neck splodge and she kissed the top of my head and then we both pulled back awkwardly like neither of us knew what had overcome us.

'Bye bye, Kit Kat,' I said.

'Bye bye, Popsicle,' she said. Then I walked out of the front doors of Paradise Vision and sat down on the bench near where the taxis drop off and pick up and I had a little cry. Not because I was sad, but because I was happy. Then, as if the day wasn't wondrous enough, I went home via McDonald's on Kilburn High Road and something lovely happened there too.

As I was walking in through the doors, concentrating very hard to remember all the stuff about ordering dinner that I learned from last time, I heard a voice shout out, 'Duchess!'

My heart nearly stopped as I knew right away it was Kwame. He was just on his way out of the door.

'I was hoping I'd see you!' he said. 'I waited an hour, but I've got to go! I promised my mother I'd be there to have some food with my auntie. I'm late already! I've got to rush.'

'Oh gosh, what a shame,' I said, trying not to

let my face dissolve into a mushy puddle. 'Another time perhaps?'

'Yes! Yes!' he said. 'Hey what about Wednesday? Here. On Wednesday. At 6pm. I'll meet you here!'

'OK!' I said.

'What's your number?' he said. 'I mean, if you don't . . . I mean, I don't want to be forward but . . . Can I have your phone number?' He was stuttering a bit. It was majorly cute.

He grabbed his phone from his pocket and typed in my number, then smiled a really amazing smile. 'See you then!' he said, then he leaned forward and kissed me on the cheek. HE KISSED ME ON THE CHEEK. Like we had just set up a proper date or something. 'See you on Wednesday, Duchess!' he said and then he vanished out of the doors.

I wanted to call Vixen, Striker or Felix immediately and tell them exactly what had happened but something stopped me. I didn't quite know what they'd say about Kwame. Kwame is so completely and utterly different to anybody that we know or hang about with. I decided that for the time being I was going to keep him a secret.

THURSDAY 22ND OCTOBER

I simply cannot believe what happened last night. I feel utterly annihilated.

My life is ridiculous. I'm ridiculous. I'm staggered by

how I was fooled into thinking things might all starting to be OK and Poppet Montague-Jones could perhaps have a normal life with happiness and laughter instead of endless days of 'boo-hoo me' and fuming under a duvet about the latest insanity which has occurred.

I'll start at the beginning:

I went to meet Kwame for my hot date last night AS ARRANGED. That date we agreed on last Saturday in McDonald's. Kwame definitely said 6pm in McDonald's on Wednesday. I'm almost ninety-nine point nine per cent sure that's what he said. He did, didn't he?

'See you 6pm on Wednesday HERE!' he said.

YES, THAT'S WHAT HE DID SAY. I know that's what he said. It wasn't 8pm. Or 5pm. He said 6pm.

I remember thinking when he said it, golly, that's totally perfect for me as I'll just have finished extra Maths with Deathbreath Douglas thirty minutes earlier, so'll have time to change in the loos and catch the bus down there.

And I remember walking up Kilburn High Street last Saturday night planning out exactly the outfit that I'd take in my bag to the Lycée to change into and trying to work out whether to do the full 34D breast enhancer pad 'sex-kitten Poppet' thing on our first date or whether to shock him with it on our second. Or, wait until our third or fourth date, which up until now I was CERTAIN there would be. And maybe even a fifth date, as I was SURE Kwame and I were going to fall madly in love.

Then I took the bus home trying to figure out a way to tell Mummy that I wasn't intending to marry Felix Hayes-Burlington from across the road, who appears every year on the *Sunday Times* 'Richest Children In Britain' list, because Felix's grandfather signed over a load of gold and art in his name just before he died – as well as a massive cash and property inheritance *after* he died.

The plain fact is that I've tried snogging Felix now on almost three occasions and each time I just didn't feel that thing that people in love are supposed to feel. That thing people talk about. That thing when you touch a person or look into their eyes and you just feel like you're crazily, mentally spirited away by intergalactic love aliens and you can't eat or sleep for imagining them.

That's what people say you're supposed to feel, isn't it? And I don't feel that with Felix. I just feel like, yes, Felix is gorgeous and sexy but he's also one of my oldest friends and when I see him I think, 'Oh yeah, let's eat cookies and gossip about people we don't like.' Yet, when I see Kwame, I DO FEEL THAT THING and we haven't even snogged each other yet.

I was trying to work out how I could possibly tell Mother this without making her wildly irate. Especially as it sounded like Kwame didn't have any money at all. I mean, he said he couldn't afford private tuition to get the grades he needed to be a doctor, didn't he? I don't really understand this I must say. I mean, tuition is quite reasonably priced isn't it? Mummy only pays about an extra three hundred pounds a week in bills to tutors. Surely everyone's parents have got a tiny amount like three hundred pounds spare for important things like their child's future?

Anyway, doesn't matter because I DON'T CARE how much money Kwame has! I don't care about money!

This was underlined to me even more when I got home last Saturday and my parents were having one of their supper parties and their friends Mimi and Hector had just showed up carrying two bottles of Cristal champagne as they all get a real kick out of drinking bubbly that is nearly a thousand pounds a bottle, and Mummy was showing them an original piece of art by the artist Jean Michel Basquiat that Daddy had brought her back from an auction in Washington DC, which was worth so much money it was being picked up by a private security firm later that evening and being transferred into the Montague-Jones family vaults.

Well, Mummy, Daddy, Mimi and Hector were all staring at the tiny scribbled drawing in its frame and marvelling about how much the tiny scribbled drawing would be worth in forty years' time, which is when I would inherit it. Turns out it will be about ten million quid, judging by the current state of art world inflation. And I'm standing with them thinking, I DON'T BLOODY CARE ABOUT MONEY! If Kwame doesn't have any money or inheritance it wouldn't matter as we would be in love!

It's safe to say I was crushing majorly on Kwame, having only met him for a total of twenty-five minutes, in McDonald's, possibly to the point of madness.

But over the last few days I've been totally mulling over whether living your life rich is more important than being with someone you truly love.

Wow, that's rather heavy isn't it? I couldn't get it out of my mind, though. I knew if I asked my mother she'd say that cash was more important, even though I know full well that Mummy married Daddy because she was crazy in love with him and he was A LOT poorer than her then. Plus Mummy was four months pregnant with Knute, which was a major scandal too. Apparently Granny was DEVASTATED when Mother first met Daddy and he confessed to Granny that his parents were called George and Susan and they worked as comprehensive school teachers and they were basically lower middle class, because my mother was and is definitely UPPER CLASS, if not higher. She's practically aristocracy!

So even though Daddy had won a place at Oxford University then set up his own television company, which won loads of TV awards and was turning over about fifteen million pounds a year, apparently Granny still screamed at Mummy, 'Jocasta, you are an utter buffoon! That man is a glorified commoner. You are marrying DOWN! You'll be counting the pennies for ever. Only fools marry for love not for money!'

And it didn't matter to Granny that Daddy's company

was a massive success and eventually he floated it on the stockmarket for two hundred million pounds, because as far as Granny is concerned my mother should have married Archduke Phillipe de Crecoix of the Hapsburg Dynasty, whose butler could have found two hundred million quid stuffed in the pocket of the Archduke's old polo jodphurs whenever he cleaned out his sporting wardrobe.

But the bottom line is that Mummy fancied Daddy to death from the moment she first met him at a party in Primrose Hill in 1988 and she followed her heart to be with him. And that's what I would have to do with Kwame too.

My head was buzzing with all of this stuff last night as I walked down the street to McDonald's, but by now I'd jumped even more steps ahead, imagining things like where Kwame and I would live when we eventually got married and, 'Gosh, this is going to mean I'll have to go with him to Africa and live in some remote place in the middle of nowhere so we can help people who are dying with fevers!' and 'Wow, I'm going to be like the first Montague-Jones woman to have a proper purpose in life!' This felt rather exciting.

So I walked into McDonald's and bought a Diet Coke and a Smarties McFlurry thingie and chose a seat near the window and I waited.

It reached 6pm and I stared at the door and kept on waiting. Then I waited some more and soon it was

6.10pm. Then it was 6.20pm and there was still no Kwame. And by this point I was feeling very anxious. But I certainly didn't want to look anxious as that would mean I would look desperate. I read in *Cosmopolitan* magazine when I was about eleven that 'men can smell desperation' a mile away and it's always worried me ever since that I am cursed with a permenantly desperate-looking face.

I checked my Blackberry for the hundreth time but there were no SMS messages, and no missed calls. Then I sent a few random emails to Vixen and Striker and Felix just to fill some time and look less lonely. Vixen had just emailed me saying she had found a 'legal loophole' in her father's rules about getting access to her trust fund, and she'd managed to withdraw thirty thousand pounds without his consent, and she'd sent it to help the street cats in Argentina. Vixen had attached an amazingly cute photo of about a hundred manky cats chowing down on a ginormous plate of what looked like tinned tuna, which was obviously a lovely thing to see and I was really very glad for Vix, but by this point it was 6.35pm and there was no sign of Kwame. And there was no message from him, even with a bad excuse, and my cheeks were feeling massively heavy up there near the eyes and I knew it would only take a minuscule amount of further sadness and I was going to start to cry.

Then suddenly a song came flooding over the speaker system and it was one that Vix and I both secretly like by

Mariah Carey called '*My All*' which is really upsetting and about being awake all night long realizing that someone doesn't love you back in the way you love them and how you'd literally cut your own arm off to spend time with them again.

Well that was it. The floodgates were well and truly opened and I started to cry. I leaped up, grabbed paper napkins and ran out of the doors because by this point I thought even if Kwame did show up late with the best excuse ever I wasn't going to let him see me with smeared eye makeup and tear-stains all down the front of my white shirt, looking like some sad cow who'd invested days and days of thought into him.

I scurried down Kilburn High Street, spotted a bus with some vaguely familiar street names on the front and waved my Oyster about, hoping to God it would take me home. We went quite a long route in almost the opposite direction at one point but I didn't care, I just sat on a seat near the back with my iPod on, not caring a damn if I got mugged or kidnapped or Rohypnolled and ransacked for a kidney, snivelling like an idiot and wiping snot down the sleeves of my Chloé moleskin jacket.

I got off about five streets from my house, then found a little wall and sat there trying to breathe deeply as I hoped it might make my eyes go down and stop being so puffy. Then I stood up, and tried to channel Striker's fierceness by putting my shoulders back and thinking, SCREW YOU, KWAME, I wasn't into you that much anyhow! I hope you catch one of your transviral bug diseases in Africa and your willy shrivels up and grows backwards into your body! Then I set off back to my house.

When I opened the front door of 1 Octavia Square, I got an odd feeling right away that something major was happening. A weird squawky sound was coming from downstairs in the kitchen that I couldn't quite place and giggles too. Then I spotted my mother's suitcases and carry-on flight luggage on the main sitting-room floor. Beside the cases was a large pink-stuffed hippopotamus with white paws.

Oh my God! I thought, 'Why does everyone keep bringing Flash and me stuffed toys as gifts when they've been away? I'm almost sixteen years old! But as I looked more closely at the hippo I realized that it had a soggy, stained ear. Like it had been chewed by a slobbery animal. There was a weird smell in the living room too. A bit like wee, or something worse, mixed with soap.

Then I heard my mother's voice downstairs saying, 'Oh aren't you beautiful! Yes you are! You are beautiful!' in a weird sloppy voice like she only uses to speak to Macbeth.

I could hear a few other voices chattering too.

I wandered down to the kitchen expecting to find my mother throwing herself a little 'Jocasta is home' party with some of her girlfriends, but what I actually found was a sight that will stay with me for ever.

My mother was standing by the sink holding a small jar of what seemed to be vegetable purée. Knute was sitting behind the kitchen table sort of smiling but also looking horrified. Mrs Minsk was holding a baby's bottle half full of milk pulling her best, 'I am not reacting to this latest event, I am only doing my job' expression.

In a highchair, in the middle of the kitchen floor, was a tiny little boy, not much older than a baby.

Oh Lords, he was gorgeous. Perfect. A mind-bogglingly beautiful little brown-skinned boy with ginormous brown eyes and a flat nose and tiny little hands with paler palms, and ears so cute I wanted to run over and give them a nibble.

'Poppet,' my mother said. 'This is Dragon! Dragon, this is your new big sister, Poppet! I managed to get him out of the orphanage in Liberia! The paperwork came through, so I just went straight there and collected him. Here, do you want to cuddle him?'

I couldn't even speak.

Mother picked him gently out of his baby chair and passed him over to me. I wrapped my arms around him and he cuddled me back and I smelled the top of his head. He smelled warm and fresh and beautiful.

'Dragon!' I said, but he didn't respond to that name at all. He just looked at me curiously then he put his hand out and touched my nose then started laughing. So then I fed him some puréed vegetable medley and he drank the other half of his bottle of milk and then we put him to bed in the room that used to be Flash's baby nursery.

Flash is away at Science Camp in Edinburgh. I can't imagine what he'll say when he gets back. Quite a lot I imagine.

So last night I slept on the sofa in Dragon's new nursery so I could watch him while he was asleep in case he woke up and was scared. I was mesmerized by him and couldn't stop thinking about where he'd come from. Plus, Dragon's nursery is one of the only places in the house that I couldn't really hear Daddy and Mummy arguing.

Funnily enough Mummy adopting a new Montague-Jones child from Africa without Daddy's consent is causing an awful amount of boo-hooing indeed.

NOVEMBER

TUESDAY 4TH NOVEMBER

Sometimes I think if I didn't have good friends like Vixen, Striker and Felix, I'd go utterly stark raving mad. They've all been completely brilliant about the arrival of Dragon from Liberia and the subsequent media fuss.

The TV, newspapers and internet have been going BERSERK about my mother's latest 'stunt', as they call it.

I decided the day after Dragon arrived that I don't want to be famous at all. I want to be the Montague-Jones child that no one knows about. No more red carpets, no appearing in my mother's *Hello!* magazine 'At home with the Montague-Jones family magazine shoots, no accompanying mother on her jaunts to Harrods in Knightsbridge with Dragon to buy baby clothes with one hundred and seventeen paparazzi following behind like angry bees.

The big problem with being famous is that you can't turn it off when it suits you. My mother loves being in magazines and newspapers when she's promoting, say, her 'Absolutely Jocasta Wall Fabrics – the world's most exclusive wallpapers', but it isn't so great right now when her Botoxed face is splashed on every front newspaper cover alongside horrible headlines saying things like:

KITTEN'S MOTHER IN AFRICAN CHILD
SNATCH SCANDAL.

And,

MONTAGUE-JONES NEW ADDITION 'DISTRESSED
AND HOMESICK' SAYS INSIDER.

Now, I must say, I'm possibly one of Mummy's harshest critics but even I know this Dragon 'being distressed' is complete and utter POPPYCOCK. Dragon doesn't seem in the remotest bit 'homesick'! I spent four hours with Dragon yesterday rolling around on a cashmere rug, feeding him the finest organic puréed fruit, watching Baby Einstein DVDs on our forty-two inch Sony Bravia TV and pushing him about in a buggy from Harrods toy department. Dragon giggled his head off all the time and slept like he was comatosed from 7pm right through until 7 this morning letting out tiny happy little snores. At NO POINT did I ever hear Dragon whimpering to be taken back to the AIDS orphanage as he was missing the mattress and the bed bugs. But I can see why the newspapers are slagging Mummy for sort of trampling over all the official rules and regulations to bring Dragon home in the first place. But that's just what it's like when you're mega-rich isn't it?

If someone tells you that you can't do something, well when you're rich you just go away and think, Who can I pay who will let me do it?

It's like when Kitten's friend Stephanos knocked over that old lady when he was drink-driving in Chelsea. Well, if he'd been someone normal he would have lost his driving licence and gone to prison, but because Stephanos's father is absolutely rolling in dosh, not to mention hugely high up at the Greek Foreign Embassy in London, well he sort of paid some people and the police didn't do anything about it. That's just what happens when you're rich.

Granny says that's the way its been for ever, especially for the British monarchy and their relatives, because, as she always reminds us, we are chosen by God.

'The MADDENING thing is, Poppet,' Mummy fumed this morning, 'is that all I'm doing here is something GOOD. But people still seek to destroy me at every point! DESTROY ME WITH LIES!'

Mummy had just been reading a feature in the *Daily Mail* newspaper which said that: 'Jocasta Montague-Jones has attracted widespread criticism (this was true), for paying off Liberian officials (true) to bring an orphaned baby home to Hampstead (true) without discussing it fully with her husband James (true) or her children Kitten Calypso, Knute Hadrian, Flash Niagara or Poppet Zanzibar, who were all deeply shocked by the move (also true). The paper also said that her daughter, infamous socialite Kitten, was reported to be bewildered and saddened by the adoption as her mother had only visited her on one occasion during her ongoing stay in rehab and had failed to mention the baby (TRUE TRUE TRUE! Mother's trip to see Kitten did more harm than good. It was worse than the tough love scheme!).

'What part of this isn't actually true?' I said to Mummy this morning as I was eating my porridge before school.

'Well, they say I'm forty-seven for a start and I'm bloody not! I'm forty-four!' tutted Mummy.

'I think that's because,' said Flash, being helpful, 'you said you were thirty-seven for ages, Mummy, when you were actually a lot older. I think they're getting their own back.'

'Thank you, Flash,' said Mother through gritted teeth. 'You're very clever to remember that.'

I could tell she wanted to tell Flash to go and get ready for school and stop being so good at remembering bad stuff, but we're all trying to be as nice as possible to Flash right now as his annoyance about Dragon has been plain to see. He wouldn't speak to any of us for an entire week when Dragon first arrived, but then I had a little word with him and asked him if he'd help us out by teaching Dragon some more words because Dragon was only little and not that many people had played with him in his old home so he was a bit behind other kids.

Well Flash LOVED this idea and has been teaching Dragon things ever since. Dragon has already mastered 'moon', 'train', and a word that sounds a lot like 'Maccapacca'. I'm starting to worry we're going to end up with another Flash on our hands. This would be a lot to deal with.

'The thing I simply can't understand,' said my mother, banging her hands down on the copy of the *Daily Mail,* 'is how they get all this information? How do they know about the Thomas the Tank engine buggy and the nursery with the sky blue ceiling?'

'I have absolutely no idea,' said Flash, wandering off sharpish.

When I left the house, there were five people sat on our front doorstep holding paper coffee cups and cameras. I covered my face with a scarf and my schoolbag and walked down the steps.

Someone came in close with what looked like a video camera, so I said in my plainest voice, 'I do not give you permission to film me. I do not give you permission to film me.' Kitten once told me to do this if I think I'm being filmed as at least it makes the person who filmed you look bad when they post it on the internet. Plus a lot of newspapers won't buy if for their websites as it makes them look bad too. I jumped into the back of the people-carrier and was relieved to see Cyril driving as he's just so chilled out he makes even the maddest situation seem calmer.

'How is the new arrival?' asked Cyril.

'Oh he's good!' I said. 'Well he's better than good, he's amazing.' I was grinning now just thinking about Dragon. It's difficult not to grin when you think of Dragon.

'They're taking him to buy him more new clothes today. He's grown out of loads of the stuff they bought him a few weeks ago, now he's getting fed properly.'

'My Lord,' said Cyril, 'that child has been dropped into heaven! It's a wonderful thing what your mother has done. The Lord will repay her.'

I couldn't believe Cyril said that. Nobody else was saying that.

We collected Vix and Striker and set off for school, with Vixen yaddering about this new boy who was chasing her called Hugo who was the younger brother of a friend of HRH Prince Harry's. Meanwhile Striker was talking about leaving school as soon as possible as she wants to move to Brooklyn in New York and start a squat new-rave band and maybe run her own music blog. I was just sitting there in the middle of them both staring out the window as we crawled along in traffic jams thinking, gosh this journey takes ages. I'm sure we could get there quicker if we went there by bus.

At the Lycée, Vixen and Striker were completely amazing, acting like my bodyguards all day long and if anyone even tried to ask me an awkward questions about Dragon, one of them would say, 'Look can we just change the subject? Poppet wants at least some of her private life to be private, doesn't she?' And at one point when Blitzen made a horrible snidey comment about the Montague-Joneses being a 'very modern little rainbow family', Striker turned round to Blitzen and told her to 'bloody shut her stupid mouth'.

Everything went very silent in Maths when Striker said that. Blitzen looked utterly shocked and then totally furious. She opened her mouth to say something else but Striker just glared at her as if to say, 'GO ON, BLITZEN, PUSH ME A BIT FURTHER, TRY ME.'

The morning dragged on for ever and the lunch hour dragged on even longer and the afternoon lasted about twenty-seven months and eventually the bell rang and we were allowed to go home. However as Vixen, Striker and me all plodded out of the front gates towards the people-carrier again something very exciting and unexpected indeed happened. I just had my hand on the back door handle going to open it when suddenly a hand tapped me on the shoulder and a voice said, 'Duchess!'

I almost jumped out of my skin. It was Kwame! Kwame was standing right in front of me looking massively happy to see me. I was totally weirded out. I started to grin and then I realized what a total pig he was and I was really very cross.

'Oh my dayz!' he said. 'I found you. I finally tracked you down!'

I stared at him. My mouth opened then closed again. All I could think about was sitting in McDonald's alone then crying on the bus home. THIS PIG STOOD ME UP.

'Well I was quite easy to find a few weeks ago,' I said. 'I was in McDonald's at 6pm remember! Like you asked me to be! And you didn't turn up. And you didn't call!

And you've never called since. Not that I care, because I don't, but that was totally jolly rude. You're a ruddy big pig by the way!'

Vixen and Striker were staring at this whole drama looking utterly confused.

'Who the heck is that?' said Striker to Vixen.

'I've absolutely no ruddy idea,' said Vixen. 'Gosh, isn't he tall?'

I looked at my two friends. Striker was leaning back getting a closer look at Kwame's bottom, which was looking particularly pert in his navy jeans, then Vixen nudged her with an elbow and she jumped and said, 'Ooh, hello, yes, POPPET, WHO IS YOUR FRIEND? DOES HE WANT A LIFT ANYWHERE?'

I shook my head and put my hand up as if to say, 'NOT NOW.'

'I lost your number!' Kwame said. 'My phone got robbed. I was mugged.'

I looked at him, he didn't seem to be lying.

'I got mugged walking through the park on my way to meet you,' Kwame said. 'Two guys punched me in the face and they took my wallet, then they tried to take my phone but I wouldn't give them it as it had your number in it, then one of them did this. Look.'

He pulled up his sleeve and there was a cut. Like a mark with a stanley knife or something, it had three stitches holding it together.

'Oh my gosh, Kwame,' I said. It was horrible.

'And it was bleeding loads. So I had to go to the hospital,' he said. 'And I tried to work out a way to call McDonald's but I was losing quite a lot of blood. So we missed each other.'

Vixen and Striker had got into the car by now as they didn't want to look like they were earwigging, which they totally were as Striker had wound the electric window down and I could see the outline of her ear clamped against the glass.

'Poppet, you get in car now, we need to go,' he said. giving Kwame a filthy look.

'Give me a minute!' I said.

'We need to leave now,' Voychek said. 'Look at the traffic!'

Voychek got back in the car and slammed the door. I stared at Kwame, remembering how gorgeous and utterly lovable he was all over again.

'So, how did you find me?!' I said.

'I've been sitting outside schools all over the area,' he said, laughing a little bit. 'I must have looked like a right perv. But after the third school I thought, oh what am I thinking? Duchess must be at the Lycée with a voice like she's got.'

I smiled when he said that, my cheeks were starting to blush. Just then, the electric window slid down properly and Striker said, 'Look, sorry Poppet's friend who she was supposed to meet at McDonalds who I have been told NOTHING ABOUT. I mean what am I these days Pops?

Am I on the top of your TELL NO NEWS list? But anyway, for Christ's sake get in the car as the driver is having a nervo breakdown.'

'I've got to go,' I said. I really, really didn't want to go. Damn Voychek!

'Meet me again!' he said. 'This time I'll show up! I promise. I'll not leave my flat from now until our meeting so I won't give anyone a chance to mug me!'

I looked at him. There was no way I could say no. I would have run away right there and then to be with him.

'Where?' I said.

'Saturday, 1pm, do you know the smoothie place that does all the cakes about ten doors down from McDonald's – Mario's?'

'Yes.' I said, mightily relieved. Of course I did. Mario's actually sold carbonated water with a fruit infusion and no one tried to stuff rancid gherkin in my dinner. I was somewhat of a regular.

'Meet me there! Give me another chance!' he said. 'OK,' I said. '1pm at Mario's Smoothies.'

'1pm at Mario's Smoothies!' he said, then he looked at me then he smiled really broadly, then he cupped my face with both his hands and he kissed me on the forehead. I thought I would nearly fall over.

I slid into the back of the car, where everyone was waiting. They'd all clearly missed the kissing incident thank God. I felt high as a kite, like I'd just inhaled love gas, but Voychek killed that moment by saying, 'What you doing talking to him, Miss Poppet? It's not good.'

'What do you mean?' I said

'Black boy hanging about school gates,' he said. 'He look like drug dealer.'

Striker and Vixen sort of gasped when he said that, but they didn't know what to say. I didn't either. I wanted to go absolutely totally mental and yell at him and then yell at his boss and get him fired for being a complete racist, but I also knew that Voychek has a wife and three children and if he lost his job then it would be very bad for them. My mind was spinning with all of this. Plus if I complained to Mother about Voychek then she'd want to know everything about Kwame and how exactly I had met him. This would cause even more carnage.

'He's not a drug dealer, Voychek!' I said, angrily. 'He's my friend and he's going to be a doctor and I'll thank you to keep your opinions to yourself from now on.'

Voychek stared ahead as if he simply couldn't hear me.

The car journey home was very quiet indeed. Of course, the moment Vixen and Striker and I were all back in our bedrooms, we were all on MSN typing like crazy with fingers of fury as the girls wanted to know every single detail I was willing to tell about 'the mega hot black boy who was going to be a doctor.'

SATURDAY 8TH NOVEMBER

Today was definitely one of the best days of my entire life ever. I simply knew it would be as I was walking down Kilburn High Street today pushing the Bugaboo Chameleon pram with Dragon in it, when the sun popped out and shone down on us both even though it's now November.

'Sunny!' I said to Dragon. He smiled at me and we both pointed upwards. 'Zun!' he said, then we both laughed. I know it was possibly an odd thing to do, taking Dragon with me to meet Kwame, but at the time it felt like a totally natural choice. Dragon and I had been together all morning having a wholly agreeable time playing 'I am a horse', because Dragon currently thinks horses are the best thing EVER after having watched Mummy and Pearl go riding last Thursday.

I'd been galloping about the nursery since 7am going 'Whinnnny' and 'Clip clop clip clop' and pretending to eat invisible carrots until Dragon was nigh on hysterical with giggles and by midday, I'd decided I didn't want to leave him behind in his nursery.

Mummy was away for the weekend on business and Daddy was in Moscow setting up a new TV station and everyone else in my family was either 'protesting at climate camp', 'at a gifted children's daygroup' or 'in rehab' so suddenly I thought, Why don't I just take Dragon with me on my adventure? After all I am his big sister. Surely that's better than being with one of his nannies? Then I thought, Maybe Dragon would like to see the world outside of Octavia Square and the back of a chauffeur-driven car? Maybe he'd like to taste a Smoothie or a spoonful of McFlurry? Then I thought, 'Maybe Dragon needs to go out and see bits of the real world and then he'll never be as terrified as I was the day I took my first bus.

I told Dragon's day nanny, Rosalla, that I was taking Dragon for a walk in his buggy and she should get him ready to leave ASAP. Rosalla looked delighted, like it was the best thing she'd heard all week. I checked out of the bay windows. No paparazzi at all. Perfect. In no time at all we'd set off.

We took the bus to Kilburn High Street and a nice Muslim man in a long gown helped me pick up the buggy and put it up the bus step so I could show my Oyster. At the other end, a man in scruffy jeans who looked like someone Mummy might get in at our house to do some painting, helped me carry Dragon's pram off.

People are actually quite kind in the outside world and not half as mean and savage as I was led to believe by people like Mummy and Blitzen.

Then we headed towards Mario's Smoothies and I was thinking to myself, Kwame, if you're not here this time my friend, then I shall never EVER think about you ever again. END OF STORY. But I was fretting for nothing because I walked into Mario's and Kwame WAS there! Sitting on one of the tall stools at the side of the café, reading a copy of *New Scientist*, wearing a black hooded top, navy blue jeans and clean white Reeboks. He looked beautiful. He saw me and his face lit up, then he saw the pram I was pushing and I could tell he nearly fell backwards off his seat.

'Hello!' I said.

'Hello Duchess!' he said, 'You've . . . I didn't . . . that's your . . .'

'It's my brother,' I said.

'I see,' said Kwame, getting down off his stool, then kissing my cheek and then looking down into Dragon's buggy, then looking up at me again seeming utterly confused.

'He's your brother?' Kwame said, putting his brown hand out and shaking Dragon's tiny little brown hands. Dragon's eyes widened when he saw Kwame and he giggled a bit. 'All right little man!' Kwame said. Then he looked at me and asked, 'Is your step-dad African?'

'No,' I said. 'I haven't got a step-father. My daddy is from Leicester. He's totally white though. Well it's hard to know what colour he is, he's quite hairy.'

It was sort of fun keeping Kwame guessing.

'This isn't your brother!' giggled Kwame.

'He is my brother! Absolutely true!' I laughed.

We both stood staring at each other. Kwame has the most beautiful brown eyes especially when he's thinking deeply. Then he whispered so Dragon couldn't hear, 'Is he adopted?'

'Yes!' I whispered back, 'He's from Liberia.'

'Amazing,' said Kwame, 'I'd like to go to Liberia one day. Work there or maybe just travel. Hey shall I get us both a smoothie? And a slice of cake that we can share? Does your brother like cake? What's his name?'

'He loves cake!' I said. 'Oh and he's called Dragon.'

'Dragon,' said Kwame, raising an eyebrow. 'Like a little monster or something.'

'Exactly like a little monster,' I said. 'A good monster though.'

'Well obviously,' said Kwame, disappearing off to the counter.

We had an amazing afternoon, just the three of us, kicking about doing nothing much. Kwame knew about a little play park not far from the High Street with swings and a slide and a sandpit and it was really incredibly busy with about forty other children whose parents were all from different types of places. White kids, Asian kids, African kids, Polish kids. I tried to imagine Mummy's face if she found out I'd been taken to a place like this. I couldn't help smiling. Mummy is so narrow-minded really.

We let Dragon out of his buggy and let him toddle about a bit, but you seriously have to keep an eye on him as he's quite fast when he gets running and he just goes WOOOOOOOOOOSH and shoots off into a crowd and you're like 'WAAAAAAAAAH! Where is he?'

Kwame and I were chatting about school and about

TV and about music and about celebrities, at which point I got rather nervous that Kwame might have heard of Kitten and assume I was exactly like my sister. But to my tremendous relief, Kwame admitted that he never ever reads celebrity gossip mags as he thinks they're a waste of time and money. This meant he's possibly never heard of Kitten! Hurrah!

However, Kwame does watch *EastEnders*, because his mum loves it, and when I told him that I'd never been to Walford and couldn't find it on the tube map, Kwame burst out laughing.

'You do know Walford isn't real don't you, Poppet? *EastEnders* is just a soap opera.'

So I laughed loudly too and said, 'Of course I do. I was just joking about thinking it was a documentary!' But inside my mind was racing and I was thinking OH MY GOD, THAT'S HOW THEY GET ALL THAT AMAZING FOOTAGE! IT'S NOT REAL, IT'S JUST ACTORS! I am so hideously dim sometimes.

I kept the subject off speaking about my family, except to say that I lived with my parents near to Kilburn. Mostly I asked him about his family instead. Kwame lives with his mother and his big sister in a flat near to Kilburn High Street. He didn't say where exactly. He was the top of his class at infant and junior school and he's now at Thamesmoore Park Comprehensive. I couldn't help sort of gasping out loud when he mentioned it as it's meant to be terribly scary. In fact when we were growing up, every time Mummy and Daddy had an argument about money, Mummy would scream 'FINE THEN, let's pull all the children out of decent school and save money by sending them to Thamesmoore Park! They can all be stabbed or dead from drugs by Year Eleven without a bloody GCSE between them!'

I didn't tell Kwame this. I imagine he sort of knew his school was rough, bearing in mind he's been ruddy mugged and cut with a knife last month! In fact, I made a serious mental note not to tell him anything Mother says, ever, as I don't think he would agree with any of it. Kwame seems to have some quite strong ideas about the rich and the poor and how unfair life is and that's why he wants to go out to Africa when he's a doctor and help them.

'It's not fair that little boys like Dragon are dying of malaria, Poppet,' Kwame said. 'Malaria isn't that difficult to control. There's drugs to prevent it and you can get these amazing anti-bug nets to sleep under so the mosquitos can't bite you. The anti-malaria packs only cost a couple of pounds each per child.'

'Oh, wow, that's OK then! What's the problem? Why can't the mothers just buy their kids the malaria tents themselves, then?'

'Well, they haven't got any money.'

'Oh . . . OK . . . Well, can't the government just give everyone one. I mean what's more important than being alive? I mean two pounds is ruddy nothing!'

'The governments have no money either. And when they do they don't give it away. It's quite complicated Poppet,' said Kwame quietly.

'Oh,' I said. I thought for a while as we sat watching Dragon running about in the grass pretending to be a horse. 'So, little kids like Dragon are dying like right now, of stuff that is totally curable and no one is doing anything about it?'

'Yes.' Kwame nodded.

'How can that be allowed?'

'I don't know,' said Kwame. 'It just is.'

I sat on the park bench and thought about the hundreds of pounds' worth of Cristal champagne my parents and Hector and Mimi can polish off as a sociable drink before dinner. It didn't make me feel very good. I made a decision in my head there and then that if I didn't do anything with my life, I'd try to make things in the world a little bit fairer. I wasn't sure how, but I knew this is what I wanted.

Kwame and I walked back to the High Street as I had to take Dragon home and give him some milk and his dinner. Plus he'd already had his nappy changed once in a public mother and baby room in a smelly park toilet and believe me, the experience wasn't a pleasant one for any of us. It was disgusting in there.

As we walked to the bus stop, Kwame held my hand and we walked along slowly chattering and I felt so totally happy that not even the odd dirty look of older people who saw a white girl and a black boy and a black baby walking along being happy could dampen my mood. I think a lot of people are racist and they don't even know themselves that they are. I bet they're the same people lying in hospital one day with a fever begging Kwame to make them better.

We reached the bus stop and Kwame and I swapped phone numbers properly, then we held hands for a while and looked at each other, then he wrapped his arms around my waist and put his face towards mine and he kissed me. A proper kiss, with mouths open and tongues moving and he didn't clash against my brace and all the time my heart was going WOW WOW WOW WOW WOW.

Then I got on the bus and he helped me lift Dragon's pram on to the step and I put Dragon on my knee so he could wave at Kwame. Kwame waved back and then put his hands in hs pocket and walked off smiling.

Oh my gosh, I absolutely ruddy love him.

THURSDAY 20TH NOVEMBER

I haven't written down any of my thoughts and feelings for days. I just can't at the moment. The thing is, I feel like an utter buffoon whenever I try to write anything down about Kwame as I go all candy-floss brained and airy-fairy and lovey-dovey and I start sounding like Vixen does when she falls madly in love, which she does with surprising regularity for one so outwardly cool, although her love rarely lasts longer than eight whole days before she's dying to be single again and not being pestered by text messages every twenty minutes.

But I totally love the being 'pestered by text messages every twenty minutes' part!

At school, I sit in Maths with my phone turned on to silent mode, dreaming up innovative and convincing excuses to put my face in inside my bag and check the screen of my Blackberry, and if there is a message from Kwame, well, my heart goes BASH! BASH! BASH! CLUNK! CLUNK! CLUNK! and all the blood swirls about in my ear canals and then I come up from underneath the desk looking like someone has drawn a clown's mouth on me!

Then, when I get asked for the next number in the linear sequence: 19 . . . 36 . . . 98 . . . well, the answer to that would be 'Kwame'. Kwame divided by the root square of Kwame equals more lovely Kwame. That's all the answers I know or will ever need to know in this lifetime.

THANK YOU VERY MUCH, DEATHBREATH DOUGLAS.

I feel like everything in my life is completely idyllic right now. I have a gorgeous, new baby brother. Kitten has apparently turned quite a dramatic corner in rehab and may be coming home very soon. Daddy is back based in London permenantly now until after Christmas. And

Mummy is going through an 'earth mother' stage with Dragon and Flash and insisting on being around and even cooking us all the occasional dinner (and oh, Jesus, it doesn't taste very good but at least she's trying).

And best of all, better than everything in the entire planet. POPPET ZANZIBAR MONTAGUE-JONES HAS A BOYFRIEND! A real-life, living boyfriend!

Not a made-up boyfriend like the one from Canada that I had in Year Nine when everyone at Lycée was claiming to have 'met someone and lost their virginity during the summer holiday' (they hadn't). So I claimed I'd met a boy called 'Curtis' in Vancouver while Kitten and I were on trip with Mummy, and Curtis was a male model and a pop star, yet I didn't have any pictures of him as he suffered from acute camera shyness.

Vixen and Striker still ruddy ask me how he is now!

'Oh,' I say, 'we don't speak any more. It was a mad passionate wham bam thank you ma'am affair. More like perfect movie love than real love. But I shall never forget him though EVER!'

Then I pretend I can't say any more as I'm becoming emotional. One day I'll tell them the truth.

I'm so glad Vixen and Striker know the truth about Kwame as having to keep him secret from my parents is killing me.

Not that I mind lying to my parents. God no, all the Montague-Jones children lie to our parents. It's more that I keep almost tripping myself up by forgetting the lies.

Like last week when Kwame and I went to his local cinema – Vue or Vule, or something – to watch *The Bell that Never Tolls*, well it was so amazingly good that I almost told my mother about it within half an hour of walking back into the kitchen. I had to stop slap bang in the middle of the sentence and then rewind and make it sound like I WANTED to go and see the movie in the future.

Of course, my mother being bloody 'earth mother' Montague jumped in and said, 'OH HEAVENS, POPPET, how divine. You, me and Kitten can go and see it, can't we? Or we can get Daddy to book the screening room at Soho House and we can have our own girls' party with nibbles and someone in to do our nails!'

'Yes, that would be lovely,' I said, trying to smile. 'I can't wait.'

I'm in an ultra-enormously difficult position now with this whole Mummy/Kwame thing. It's not that I think Mummy wouldn't like Kwame, I think she would like him a lot eventually, as what's not to love? But I know she would be jolly angry about all the sneaking about I've done so far. And she'd probably be concerned about the school Kwame went to and she'd start saying I was going to get stabbed if I hung about with him, especially as he's been slashed once too. (Kwame must NEVER tell Mummy that he got mugged for his phone and cut with a knife. This will only make things worse for us.)

There's also the fact that Kwame doesn't seem to have much money either. Mummy will say he's trying to get at my money, which he completely isn't as he doesn't even know anything remotely about my money. I pretend I haven't got any money when I'm with him and believe me it is JOLLY HARD!

Mummy won't believe that, though. Mummy says that's why rich people should only really make firm friendships with other rich people as then they know for sure they're true friends and not just with them for their money.

Mummy says she's never met a poor person who was really that interesting anyhow, in the longterm, as they don't go anywhere or do anything and it's not like you can talk to them about wine or nannies or property.

This makes Mummy sound like a total snob, which she completely isn't.

Oh honestly. Who am I trying to fool? My mother is the worst snob ever.

Anyway, BIG NEWS today on the Poppet/Kwame front. I'm going to meet his mother!

My plan, if it all goes well and she doesn't hate me and ban Kwame from seeing me, is to be mega-brave and introduce him to my mother and father. And everyone will get along swimmingly and with grand aplomb and we'll all put our differences behind us and it will be like a Coca-Cola advert, and we'll all be laughing and there may even be a small dance-routine involving us all out in the square tap-dancing and life will be ruddy completely wonderful.

I can just feel it.

SUNDAY 3RD NOVEMBER

I've been thinking a lot about truth today. Truth is sort of important in relationships I'm beginning to figure out. If anything it's the most important thing. I've been thinking this today as I realize there are lots of things Kwame still doesn't know about me. It's not that I've been lying to him. I have never ever lied to him. But I've been side-stepping neatly around the truth. Or avoiding the subject completely.

Kwame doesn't know I am Poppet Montague-Jones from Octavia Square, Hampstead. He thinks I am Poppet Jones who lives in a small house on the outskirts of Kilburn.

He doesn't know I am eighty-seventh in line to the throne, or that I will receive a trust fund of around ten million. He just thinks I must have an OK allowance, which means I sometimes have a spare ten-pound note if we want popcorn at the cinema. He thinks my father works for the digital TV company Spike TV in the computer department, even though Daddy actually runs the company and about twenty-three other Spike companies in different countries and also has the majority share in the Forbes-Ellise luxury hotel chain as well as owning tonnes of property all over London.

I didn't lie about what Daddy does. I just didn't tell Kwame very much. Kwame doesn't know that the sculpting I was 'kidding' about is actually real sculpting

216

and is currently being exhibited in the ICA just off the Mall beside Buckingham Palace, and Mummy took all the Montague-Jones family to Gordon Ramsay's new restaurant after the opening and he brought up a 1984 bottle of Chateau Mar de Baux to celebrate my arrival into the art world.

Kwame doesn't know any of this at all. I've been hiding things that I don't know if he'll understand until I feel I know him better.

And now I find out Kwame hasn't been telling me the truth either. I found that out tonight. I'm not mad at him all. He's not been lying. He's just been doing exactly what I have. Sort of making the facts less hard to swallow.

I still adore him. I will do whatever.

So I set off tonight to meet Kwame's mother.

I was terrified, to be quite honest. I've never really met any boy's mother before. Well, except Felix's mother, but she's known me for ever and at one point Felix and I even shared a nanny. Being at Felix's house is almost as comfortable as being at my house. (Golly, this reminds me, I must make an effort to see Felix this week. I'm sure he's avoiding me. I can't think what I've done either.)

Anyway, I agreed to meet Kwame outside McDonald's and then we'd get the bus to his home near to Kilburn High Street together. We jumped on a bus and it set off trundling along down the long road that would eventually lead almost back to my house, except it doesn't, it sweeps off into the housing estates.

As the bus was letting people on and off I kept saying, 'Are we getting off soon?'

And Kwame kept saying, 'Another few stops. Another few minutes.'

And soon we were getting closer and closer to the area of housing estate that always gives me the complete fear and I started thinking, Oh my gosh, I hope Kwame doesn't live anywhere near here as we're almost near the Cottingham! But I didn't want my face to change so I just held his hand and concentrated on my breathing. But then we drew closer, stop by stop, to the three tower blocks and the tiny children's play park and the horrible broken down little hall that has kids outside sitting on the steps with their death dogs, smoking joints, and inside my head I was screaming, NOOOOOOOO NOT THE COTTINGHAM!!!

And then Kwame said, 'Come on, Duchess, this is where we get off.'

I froze for a moment.

Kwame wanted me to get out of the relative safety of the bus. I didn't have a stab vest on and I was idiotically wearing a diamond ring worth half a million that once belonged to the King of Monaco!

'OK,' I said, pretending everything was completely cool.

I stepped on to the pavement, which was cracked with the remnants of dog poo smeared on it, then we walked through the gates and towards Block C of the Cottingham's three apartment blocks.

Well soon some of the kids hanging about outside the community hall were shouting, 'WOOOO-HOOO! Dr Kwame is with a woman!'

I felt like shouting, 'Run, Kwame! Run! Feral children! They may have Mad Cow Disease!'

But Kwame just laughed his deep laugh and said, 'Oh come on, Duchess, let's go and say hello.'

We wandered over to a group of kids, me hiding behind Kwame's legs. Some of them were really tiny, like only about seven years old, but they were really really gobby and started asking Kwame all sorts of personal questions about me but he took it in good spirits and said, 'OK, pipe down, right, who is playing football on Sunday morning then? We need two teams of seven. I'll be in the hall at 10am sharp.'

And the little boys looked really happy when he said that.

One little boy with light brown skin and glasses with a broken side said, 'The floor is all slippy at the moment tho isnit, Kwame, the holes in the roof is all leaking again. Get me?'

'Well I'll see if we can get some more buckets to catch the water,' said Kwame, smiling.

And then a really big, white girl in jeans so low I could see her bum crack appeared out of the hall doorway and said in what sounded like a totally Jamaican accent, 'Hey,

Kwame, you need to be all out of here by noon on Sunday max 'cos we doing bingo and a pie for the pensioners, then the youth group have booked it 'cos they's practising their dancing. They're going on *X-Factor* they reckon, innit.'

Kwame laughed at the *X-Factor* bit and then he said, 'Oh my dayz, Sunday is gonna be a busy day then. Did the council call about the roof at all?'

'Nah,' said the girl. 'They ain't called back once and I left them five messages. 'Ere, anyway, iz that your woman then, or what, innit?'

Kwame turned round and put his arm around my shoulder. 'Yes,' he said, 'this is my woman. But I think she'd rather be called Poppet.'

'Aight, Poppet,' smiled the girl. 'I'm Shazzalla.'

'Hello,' I said. My voice sounded like my Mother's. 'Enchanted to . . .' I began to say and then I coughed instead and shut up.

We went to Kwame's flat to meet Mrs Kobina. Kwame lives on the seventeenth floor of Block C and the lift wasn't working so we got out after ten floors as I was scared it was going to stop working altogether and we'd be trapped.

Kwame says that this often happens and that's why he's got such strong legs as he always walks it too. The stairways were dark, and had graffiti all over them, and they were pretty bloody scary, although everyone seemed to know Kwame and say hello to him as we passed them.

I was feeling sort of glum by then, but then we got inside Kwame's mum's flat and the mood changed entirely.

You would have never known you were in the Cottingham. Kwame's flat was tiny. Like I can't believe how tiny. I mean the size of our living-room at home. And it was ultra-clean and very organized with a place for everything and every surface polished.

An amazingly strong smell of meat roasting hit me as I walked through the doors. On the living-room shelves were rows of Kwame's trophies for sports, and framed certificates for amazing things he had done during his life, like pass a first aid course and raise some cash for charity. I was almost certain Kwame's mother had not bribed anyone for any of them.

Then, as we heard Kwame's mother coming out of her bedroom where she had been talking on the phone, Kwame turned to me and said, 'OK, no swearing, no mentioning anything like smoking or drinking. Oh, and she loves God, so no taking the mick out of the big man, right.'

'Right!' I said, making a mental note of all of that. And then the door opened and in walked Mrs Kobina and she looked at me and said, 'Oh my lord in heaven above! She's a white girl!'

So I looked at her in horror and thought, crap, is that a problem? Because I can't ruddy do anything about that one!

Well, Kwame had his face clutched in his hands at this

point and he said, 'Mother, this is Poppet.'

'Hello!' I said, putting out my hand, 'Enchanted to meet you!'

Well, she walked across smiling and put a hand out and shook mine very warmly and said, 'Hello, hello! And you speak like the Queen! Enchanted to meet you too! Ooh aren't you a slim little thing too. You need fattening up!'

'Mother!' said Kwame. 'Can you stop saying everything that comes into your head the minute you think it. Like we talked about!'

'Ha ha ha!' Mrs Kobina laughed. 'I can't help but speak the truth, I never knew she was white! I thought she may be mixed but not white!' she said.

I held out my arm. 'Well I'm not white. I think it's like porridge colour,' I said.

Kwame's mother is about the same age as my mother. She has a voice that is quite cockney but with definitely more bits of African in it then Kwame's accent, especially when she says some phrases. She is rather beautiful and you can see by pictures around the living-room that she was mega-pretty when she was eighteen.

'Right, we're having lamb stew. We eat at 7pm on the dot and then I can find out all about Her Royal Highness, Poppet!' she said, disappearing into the kitchen.

Tonight turned out to be rather good fun indeed. Possibly not for Kwame, who perhaps didn't want me to see a photo of him having a bath in a bucket aged five with his willy on display. And maybe didn't want me to hear about how very, very, very proud she is of him and how he is going to be a doctor and save children in Africa. And about how Kwame's dad basically walked out on them when Kwame was two and his sister was four and never ever saw them again and how at one point they were so poor they were living on food handouts from the church. But that's what Kwame's mother is like. Ask her a question and she'll tell you the truth.

So I found out practically all of the truth about Kwame tonight, but it didn't make me dislike him. It just made me adore him even more.

TUESDAY 25TH NOVEMBER

Oh my gosh. The worst thing ever has happened tonight.

EVER EVER EVER EVER EVER EVER EVER EVER.

I HATE VOYCHEK. Hate him! Why did I not get him fired for being a gigantic racist when I could? Why did I care about his feelings and his life? He didn't care about mine. Now he has ruined my life for ever. I can't write anymore. I am definitely going to kill myself. That's it. It's not even a joke this time.

Goodbye world for ever.

DECEMBER

WEDNESDAY 3RD DECEMBER

I don't know what is worse, Kitten Montague-Jones my
druggy, needs-to-go-to-rehab big sister who never knows
what the hell is going on in my life and tells me to shut
my gob ten times a day, OR Kitten, who is out of rehab
and is in the house all day long every day, with a totally
clear head, thinking she knows EVERYTHING about my
life and wanting to give her opinion.

I can't believe, since she got clean, that Kiss FM have
taken her on as a resident agony aunt on their Sunday
night phone-in slot. Kitten now thinks she's a world
authority on everything: love, sex, families, drug
addiction, adoption, everything!!! This morning I had to
sit in the kitchen with her as she gave me her advice on
the Kwame Kobina fiasco.

'Well, I can't believe you could be so bloody
stupid anyway, Poppet! What the hell were you doing
hanging about the Cottingham with a boy who sells
drugs!' Kitten sighed.

'HE DOES NOT SELL DRUGS!' I roared for the
seventeenth time this week. 'He is going to be a doctor of
transviral diseases!'

'Well, Voychek says he's seen this boy hanging around

the school gates approaching people,' said Kitten, painting her toenails red as she was just off out to start filming her new work-out DVD 'The Big Mind and Body Cleanse Work Out with Kitten Montague-Jones', which is on the shelves in January.

'Kwame was approaching me!' I said. 'That's who he was approaching. Why will no one believe me.'

'But, Poppet,' said Kitten, 'he's from the bloody Cottingham! And he's African! You know what that looks like!'

'Kitten,' I said, narrowing my eyes, 'Dragon is African!'

'Oh, you know damn well what I mean,' said Kitten. 'Dragon lives with us now, so he's different. The African families on the Cottingham Estate deal drugs and do Voodoo. I saw it in the *Evening Standard*.'

'Oh, so Kwame and his mother are drug dealers and they also practise ruddy Voodoo!' I shouted. 'Gosh they must be busy bees! I don't know how he fits all this in alongside studying for NINE GCSEs and running the estate's bloody football team and helping out in the pensioner's bingo and pie afternoons.'

Kitten didn't say anything then, she just reached out and put her hand on my hand and I shut up. Tears were welling up in my eyes. I have been officially grounded with no phone and no internet access for ten days and I have gone to a very bad place indeed.

'Oh Jesus,' said Kitten, 'you love him don't you? You're totally in love.'

'Whatever,' I said.

'Yes, you are,' she said. I burst into tears then. Kitten held my hand and let me cry for a minute and then she said, 'Well if he's not a drug dealer and he doesn't do Voodoo and he's a lovely boy who runs a football team and helps old ladies to eat pies or whatever it was you're quacking on about, then why have you been hiding him?'

I looked at her then, I didn't want to say.

'Are you embarrassed about what we'll think of him?' said Kitten.

'No, not at all,' I squealed.

'Are you embarrassed of what he'll think of us?' she said.

I looked at the table. If I was to be totally honest, YES. Yes I completely was. The Montague-Jones family are so completely utterly different to everyone else I know, even in Hampstead, that I just couldn't imagine how he would react when he met them.

'Well, then,' said Kitten. 'Why don't we get this sorted out then. In my capacity as Kiss FM agony aunt, and as someone who has been through rehabilitation and really really got in touch with my inner voice and learned to seize the moment and honour each experience as it happens, while also embracing the future with a sense of positivity—'

'Kitten, I need to go to school now,' I said. 'Can you finish the sentence.'

'Oh . . . yes . . . We need to invite Kwame here to meet

Mummy and Daddy and Knute and me and Flash and Dragon and everyone. That's what we need to do.'

I totally felt like throwing up at the thought.

'That's the only way this can feasibly be sorted,' she said. 'After all, he is your ruddy boyfriend.'

'He WAS my boyfriend,' I said, sobbing again. 'That silly cow of a mother has taken my Blackberry and it's the only place I've got his number. And he can't call me. And he doesn't know where I live. And Mother has hired Voychek full time to ship me places on double-time wages so I can't even breathe without the big stupid pig writing it down on a clipboard. And Mother thinks this is money well spent, considering she didn't keep a close enough eye on you and that cost her about two hundred grand in the end, as you were supposed to go to rehab for twenty-eight days and ended up staying nearly three and a half months and smashing up Paradise Vision's furniture!'

Kitten's face didn't even flicker then, it kept its Zen-like expression.

'You seem very angry, Pops,' she said. 'Maybe you need some counselling about it. Shall I schedule you an appointment with Dr Sarzberg?'

'NO.' I said. 'I don't want to see Dr Sarzberg. I want to see Kwame!'

'OK,' said Kitten. 'Well then, we'll have to invite him over. I'll speak to Mother today and talk her into giving you your phone and SIM card back. But only on the condition that you call Kwame and tell him to come round for supper. Hey what about on the twelfth of December? Then he can come to the Octavia Square Christmas carol service in the gardens and meet everyone together.'

I thought about this. I would rather cut my hand off with an axe, sprinkle it with parmesan cheese, and eat it with a rocket salad, but it felt like I had no choice.

'OK,' I said.

'Oh, fabulous,' said Kitten. 'Holy damn, I am on fire today with advice! I must write this down for my self-help book that I'm publishing next summer! This would be a chapter all of its own.

SATURDAY 13TH DECEMBER

What on earth did I think I was doing listening to my big sister's advice? When has Kitten ever had a 'good idea' about anything?

Like that time when we were little and she decided we should take Daddy's razor and shave off our eyebrows to make us look prettier? Well it didn't make us prettier, did it, Kitten?

And the time she decided it would be a good idea to cut up Mummy's three-thousand-pound Chanel jacket and two-thousand-pound Gucci snakeskin trousers so that we could pretend to be Halloween zombies. Again, this turned out to be a very unwise move with bleak far-reaching consequences.

Yet, somehow, simply because Kitten is my big sister, and she's got a confident way of saying things, I end up doing what she says. And this is going to stop!!! Especially as she's not on drugs anymore and has three times the amount of time in her day to dream up idiotic schemes.

She was on *GMTV* this morning talking about beating drug addiction through the power of step aerobics and suggesting that the government should take to the streets of London's ghettos and hand out tracksuits and headbands to anyone who is hooked on smoking crack AND THE PRESENTER WAS AGREEING WITH HER. And then by the time her car dropped her home at Octavia Square someone from the prime minister's office was on the phone asking her to come in and add her brainpower to a special government 'think tank' on drugs. I am not even exaggerating.

So, not only is Kitten bossing ME around and bossing Flash around and bossing the people who making her fitness DVD around, she is now working for the government bossing the general public around too.

KITTEN MUST BE STOPPED.

And the first thing I'm taking out of her control is me. Especially as she has all but destroyed my relationship with a lovely, decent boy called Kwame. SHE'S DESTROYED IT. I mean DEAD. I very much doubt I will see Kwame ever again. And if you're reading this in a hundred years in the future – maybe someone like Felix's mother has found the diary in an old attic and ridden frantically across London on a Hercules shopper bicycle to 'verify that they are indeed ye olde diaries of the eighty-seventh in the line to the British throne' – well, then I will hereby present the evidence of why I know I have been dumped:

It was ruddy tough enough getting Kwame to come and meet me in the first place. Let's face it, I had gone completely missing off the radar for eleven whole days after going to meet his mother. Kwame had left tonnes of messages and texts as he was worried about me and then he started to think that I'd basically dumped him as I couldn't possibly date someone who lived in such a squalid, depressing place as the Cottingham, whose mother said everything that came into her head and showed me photos of him in the nude in a bucket with his willy out.

My first conversation with Kwame when I got my phone back was really bumpy as he sounded really depressed and a bit angry and it was only when I burst into tears crying and said, 'KWAME, THEY TOOK AWAY MY RUDDY PHONE AND INTERNET CONNECTION AND MY LAPTOP AND I'VE BEEN UNDER HOUSE ARREST!' Well, only then did he start to listen and perhaps believe that I wasn't a gigantic cow.

Then on the second phone call I said, 'Look, Kwame, they want to meet you! If you come over for supper or something then it'll make everything much better.'

So Kwame said, 'When is supper? I don't usually eat before I go to bed. Do I have to come over in my pyjamas?'

'No, supper!' I laughed. As in dinner at night, but less, y'know formal, I mean not like a dinner as such but more like something our housekeeper throws together.'

'You have a housekeeper?' said Kwame.

'Erm, no,' I said. 'Well, yes, sort of. Well, by "sort of", you understand I mean, erm, yes. Oh God, Kwame, just come over for a meal of some description or even just a mince pie as it's Christmas? Do you want to come to a carol service? Do you like Christmas carols?'

'I love Christmas carols,' he said, warming up a bit. 'I've just had the kids on the estate doing the Twelve Days of Christmas for the OAPs.'

'How did that go?!' I said, remembering again why I am crazy about him.

'Well, not so good to be honest. They get as far as the "five gold rings" part and then they love that part so much that they start getting all silly. But it's all good. They had fun. But then the roof started leaking in at the end so we had to cancel the party afterwards as the old dears were falling over.'

'Crikey,' I said. There was a silence.

'Come to the carol service here,' I said. 'It will be jolly. I promise.'

Kwame thought for a second.

'OK,' he said.

My heart was dinging and donging so merrily on high by this point that I forgot to tell him any more details. I only texted him the address earlier this evening.

So tonight, at about 6pm, Kwame was scheduled to come to 1 Octavia Square, to have a mince pie and sing a song about a robin and meet my family. However, when Mummy was agreeing to all of this and saying, 'This will be such a good way to assuage any feelings of fear I have about this situation! Bring him round and let him meet everyone!' Well, I didn't know that 6pm was also the time she had arranged a pre-carol 'Open House' session for all of the neighbours. She didn't mention this at all.

So by 6.15pm, there was no sign of Kwame but there was definitely sign of my mother, Striker's mother Paloma and Vixen's mother Ramona, all in the lounge drinking Martinis made by a bartender I'd never even seen before, chatting loudly about sex and shopping.

I seriously hoped God would strike them all down with laryngitis before Kwame showed up, especially as Paloma was saying, 'Well I say this to my clients! Sexual dysfunction is so very common in the over-40s marriage! This is why you need to work hard to SPICE THINGS UP and . . .'

By this point I'd heard enough so I went into the hallway where Kitten was on her Blackberry barking, 'I don't care what the prime minister says. I am telling him, the tracksuits and headbands for the homeless and crack-addicted plan should be actioned immediately!'

Flash was kicking a football about in the hallway saying, 'Look, Poppet, it's signed by the entire England football team to me personally! Daddy met them on an aeroplane when he flew home from Brazil!'

Meanwhile three nannies who I've never seen before were on the first-floor landing all passing Dragon about and bickering about whose turn it was to change his bum.

Then Daddy walked in and looked at the twelve-foot Christmas tree we have in the hallway and said, 'Why are the lights not working? I ship the bloody thing all the way from Norway and then she can't even organize for the sodding lights to twinkle! Jocasta what is wrong with these lights! Mrs Minsk! What is wrong with these lights!'

And my mother was shouting, 'Oh lighten up, James, and have a bloody egg-nog. It's supposed to be Christmas you gigantic grouch!'

Well then the front door bell rang and my heart jumped so I flung it open and it was Striker. Her hair was electric blue! And she was wearing a tiny little miniskirt and a boob-tube that looked like it was made of tinsel.

'Striker!' I said. 'Wow that is a, erm, big statement!'

'Damn right,' said Striker, waltzing past. 'I am all about Big Statements now. Next year is all about the Biggest Statements, Popsicle. That's what I might even call my new band. THE BIG BLOODY STATEMENTS.'

So Striker walks into the living-room and Paloma spots

her hair, and chucks an utter crap-attack and they're bickering and Paloma was saying Striker looked like an alien and Striker was saying, 'Good! That's what I want to look like! I've succeeded!'

Then the front door bell went again and this time I was SURE it was Kwame, but it wasn't it was Vix and she was snivelling a bit going, 'Is my daddy here?'

'No,' I said. 'But I think he's coming.'

'Well I am not speaking to him so keep him in a separate room. He's found out about the donation I made to the Argentinian cat fund and he's acting like a lunatic. I'm going to phone that Paradise Vision place your sister was in and see if they can come round with some of those buckly pyjamas and cart him off. Stupid man.' Vix was uncharacteristically emotional.

'Oh, Vixy,' I said and I gave her a hug. Then Striker came in and gave her a hug, and then Flash kicked the football at the Christmas tree and it reverbed and hit Mummy's ten-grand imported Tuscan antique mirror and almost nearly shattered it and then everyone was milling about sort of laughing and squabbling and being very noisy. So noisy, in fact, that I didn't hear the door bell go again and Mrs Minsk answering it.

I didn't see Kwame until he was standing in the hallway, in the middle of everyone, just staring at me with a big, wide, rather shocked-looking expression.

'Kwame!' I said. 'Everyone, this is Kwame!'

'Helllooooooo, Kwame, enchaaaaanted to meet you!'

said practically everyone, including Mummy who actually looked rather hammered and it was only 6.45pm in the evening. Do we all say 'enchanted to meet you'? Oh gosh, we actually do, I didn't even notice until now.

'Let's go and get you a drink!' I said, whisking him over to the cocktail bar.

Kwame was sort of speechless.

'I'm thrilled you came!' I whispered. 'Do you want a Martini or something? Mummy doesn't mind us boozing if it's Christmas.'

Kwame opened his mouth then closed it again, 'You live in Octavia Square, Hampstead,' he said, quietly.

'Yes, I know,' I said.

'I thought you lived on the borders of Hampstead, like in Kilburn,' he said.

'Mmm, yeah,' I said. 'Well I suppose I do, if you think about it, erm, wonkily.'

I felt a bit guilty then. Was that a really bad lie after all?

'I'm late because I was stopped by the police on the way here. About two streets away,' he said. 'They did a stop and search on me. That's why I would never ever come round here usually. It's sort of scary.'

'Oh my word,' I said. 'That's terrible! They must have thought you were a burglar.'

The moment I said that, I knew it was wrong. But then it was also the truth, even though it was a horrid truth and not one that I wanted to think about at all. I put my hand out and touched his arm. I wanted to kiss him and say everything was going to be OK, but I don't think he wanted me to.

'I know they did,' he said. 'If I walk into Octavia Square, then that's the first thing they think.'

'Well you're not a ruddy burglar!' I said. 'You're completely honest and amazing and gorgeous and clever and I adore you.'

The thing was, instead of sounding like I was telling the truth here, now I sounded like I was being patronizing. How did that happen? And I wasn't. I think Kwame is one of those people who could be prime minister if he wanted to be. He really is that special.

But just then, as if things couldn't get any worse, Vixen's father Mr Brocklehurst arrived, and he was tipsy and he was holding two bottles of Cristal champagne and he walked straight into the party and said, 'OK, Jocasta, I bought over your favourite tipple, and they charged me nine hundred quid a bottle for it as they must have seen me coming, but sod it, it's Christmas, let's get the corks out!'

Mummy cheered wildly and then Mr B said, 'I mean, hey, what's money? That idiot daughter of mine has just given thirty grand to help cats with poorly paws in Argentina.'

'Oh, shut up, Daddy!' shouted Vixen. 'Shut up!'

I turned to Kwame, but he couldn't meet my eye any more.

'I've got to go, Poppet. I'm sorry. I can't handle this. I'm sorry. I've got to go.'

So he went. My relationship with Kwame is over.

After he'd gone Felix showed up and he sat on the stairs with me while I cried and put his arm around my shoulder and said, 'If he lets you go, Poppet, he's an idiot. You're one in a million.'

He was only being nice. There is nothing remotely unique or special about me at all.

MONDAY 22ND DECEMBER

I know that deep down everyone is jolly happy about it being over between Kwame and myself. No one wants to say it out loud, though.

'Phew! Close one there! We nearly had someone from the Cottingham lurking about the house eyeing up the fine *objet d'art*. Someone who doesn't know his way round a dining table full of fish knives, soup spoons, side plates and pointy things to eat lobster with. Someone who doesn't know that gazpacho soup is meant to be vile, and meant to be served ice cold, and doesn't understand that when you have afternoon tea at Claridges there is an excessive amount of teapots and jugs of hot water and sieves and spoons that fit inside other spoons and special spoons to rest other spoons on and ONLY after half an hour of bashing about with spoons can you have the scone with jam which is the only thing you really wanted.'

No one has said this to me directly, but I can tell that's

what they're ruddy thinking. They think that Kwame and I are too different. That's why I should be with someone like Felix who can order from a sushi menu in Bloomsbury in rather decent Japanese, and has his own library and study in the basement of his house with first edition classics of his grandfather's novels that are worth about a million pounds.

People think Felix is suitable for me and Kwame simply isn't.

So, OK, I sort of accept that it is over now. I haven't got closure about it but Mummy says that she will book me in for half a dozen sessions with Dr Sarzberg after Christmas because she found that jolly helpful when we had to have our other labrador Godot put down a few years back.

I don't want any therapy. I don't want closure on Kwame. There is nothing about Kwame I want to forget. The whole thing with Kwame just taught me that there's a far bigger world outside Octavia Square and there are some jolly nice people in it really.

It also told me that the world isn't fair and it's up to me to do something about it. And really do something about it. Not just like Mummy does when she says she wants to do something about the unfair things in the world when she's having a charity luncheon but has forgotten by the time the car has dropped her home.

One thing Kwame has taught me is that 'doing stuff quietly' is a far far more amazing thing than, telling everyone you're doing stuff, then not really doing it at all.

Like Kwame and the pie and bingo afternoons in the leaky hall. If I'd never gone to the Cottingham I'd never ever have known.

OK, better stop writing now. We're just about to sit down to our annual pre-Christmas roast swan dinner which is a tradition in this house as Granny can get access to swans. I don't think normal people can eat swans, but we're not normal, are we? The Montague-Jones family are chosen by God.

WEDNESDAY 24TH DECEMBER

I'm lying in my bed wrapped up in my duvet like a Poppet sausage roll, thinking about today and everything that happened.

Christmas Day in the Montague-Jones house is always pretty special. For a start, there's a LOT of presents. Like silly presents. Silly as in so ostentatiously enormous that you don't have a clue what to say when you open the box.

Basically, in our family, we're all so horrid to each other for three hundred and sixty-four days a year that Christmas Day is the day we make it up by gifting each other idiotically expensive stuff like diamonds and sportcars and racehorses.

Or, like today, when I opened a gift from Mummy and Daddy and it was just a plain old rock in a box. 'What does this mean, Mummy?' I said.

'Well you're sixteen soon, so we decided to buy you a

tiny island. Nothing enormous. A few miles long. More like an investment really,' said Mother. 'It's in the Carribean. Maybe you could build a hotel on it one day. Or just sell it.'

'Wow,' I said, not really knowing what the correct reaction was to being given an island.

'Well it's just something for your portfolio,' Daddy added. 'You don't have to think about it at all for now. We just wanted you to have your own land.'

Then, after Flash and Dragon opened their mountain of gifts from Hamleys, and Knute had gathered up all the wrapping paper to recycle and Kitten had made the point that *she* hadn't got an island yet, and everyone had bickered a bit and then made friends again, then we told the waiting staff that we were ready to eat dinner.

I didn't feel like eating really. I haven't for weeks, but I went along with looking hungry anyway and I sat at my table place and I pulled a cracker with Mummy and took out the Tiffany teardrop necklace which was the gift inside it and put it on and wore the silly hat and tried to join in with the festive cheer.

But then just as we were about to start eating there was a ring on the front door bell. We all stared at each other. We weren't expecting anyone and Mrs Minsk was on holiday so there was no one to answer it.

'Oh, I'll have a look who it is,' I sighed.

'Spy through the keyhole first, Poppet! It could be armed robbers! Don't let anyone in!' cried Mother.

'Yeah, obviously,' I said, walking towards the door.

I opened the door without looking through the spy hole.

Standing outside on the steps was the best Christmas present I have ever had EVER.

It was Kwame.

'Kwame!' I squealed quietly. 'Happy Christmas! What are you doing here?'

'I don't know,' he said, shaking his head slowly. 'Well, I wanted to bring you a present.'

He passed me a small box wrapped in paper with Christmas pudding on it. I took it from him and opened it up. It was a plasticky glass box of chocolates. Each one was wrapped in gold paper.

'What are these?' I said.

'Ferrero Rocher!' said Kwame, giggling. 'You're a posh sort of girl, so I bought you a posh type of present.'

'Were they very expensive?' I said. I was worried he'd spent a lot of money.

Kwame shook his head and giggled like I'd said something very funny.

'Ooh, about two pound twenty,' he said.

'I love them!' I said. 'Thank you.'

We stood in silence looking at each other.

'Are you having a nice Christmas?' I said.

'Erm, well I've had better,' he said, then he sighed loudly like he was in pain. 'I miss you, Duchess.'

I looked at him and said nothing.

Thankfully I didn't scream, 'I MISS YOU TOO, I FEEL LIKE MY LIFE IS OVER!!' as that would have been neither cool or subtle.

'So the last few weeks have been sort of rubbish,' he said. 'But then something mad happened last night too.'

'Oh, what's that?' I said.

'A charity rang up Shazalla and said they'd pay for the hall roof to be fixed. The Children's Revolution, they're called. They've given me and Shazzalla thirty thousand pounds and we can access it immediately to pay builders. We can put a new kitchen in too.'

'Oh my gosh!' I said. 'How did that happen?'

'I've no idea,' he said. 'I mean Shazzalla wrote some letters off to some places months ago but we didn't hear anything. I don't know what happened. I think it was maybe my mother and all her praying.'

'It has to be,' I said, keeping my face very straight and not even letting my eyes flicker. I can't believe that whole thing went so smoothly. One call to Mr Chenowitz telling him I knew my rights about accessing my trust fund, then a quick email to The Children's Revolution, and that's all it took to turn a load of people's lives around completely.

'So, you're OK then?' I said. Kwame thought for a while.

'I'd be better if we were speaking, Poppet. I think we need to maybe try again. But with us both telling the truth this time,' said Kwame. We stared at each other a little longer, then he walked up the steps to 1 Octavia Square and he took my face in his hands and he kissed me.

'I'm in love with you, Duchess,' he said. 'And I've no idea what to do about it, but come and tell you.'

'Well I'm in love with you too, Kwame,' I said. Then we snogged some more on the steps of my house for such a long time I was sure someone in another house was probably on the phone calling 999 to say Poppet Zanzibar Montague-Jones was cannoodling with 'an African burglar'.

After a lot of snogging, Kwame wandered off in the direction of the Cottingham and I floated back inside 1 Octavia Square with a smile from ear-to-ear, and my stomach doing cartwheels, and told everyone it was some bad carol singers at the door. Then I tried to eat my Christmas dinner but all I could think about was HIM.

'I didn't tell everyone in the family that Kwame Kobina and I are officially in love and completely and utterly seeing each other again.

I didn't tell them I don't give a ruddy hoot what they feel about it. I didn't say how I've decided that from now on Poppet Zanzibar Montague-Jones's life will never be the same again. Or how I'm following my own dreams, not anyone else's. Or how I'm going to go out there into the big wide world and made a ruddy difference.

I didn't tell them any of that stuff because, after all, it is Christmas and everyone was being jolly so it would have been churlish to start a huge family row and end up all over the newspapers again.

I'm telling them first thing tomorrow.

POPPET'S GLOSSARY

A

Mr Abdul: Geography teacher. Likes oxbow lakes, maps and quacking on about the GCSEs.

Miss Alitash Abraha: Hampstead Lycée girl. Her daddy is the Ethiopian Ambassador in London. Terribly nice girl.

Mr and Mrs Mimi and Hector Adam-Short: Mummy and Daddy's close pals. Big champagne drinkers.

Master Marmaduke Adams: Godspeed Boys Academy pupil. Ruddy annoying pervert.

B

Miss Babblebrook: Equestrian tutor. Still has no sense of humour about 'the OAP picnic trampling incident.'

Bramble: famously naughty pony at Hampstead Lycée stables. Loves picnics.

Miss Miranda Brocklehurst: Vixen's aunt. Rents an amazing house every summer in The Hamptons, Long Island, New York. Loves to party.

Mr Travis Brown: Lead singer with universally adored 'space rock' band 'The Jet Fighters'. Eco Warrior. Friend of Mummy's.

Miss Flora Bryce: Hampstead Lycée girl. Her daddy drives a Saab.

C

Miss Belle Caribou: Hampstead Lycée girl. One of Blitzen Trapper's BFFs.

Miss Indira Chander: Hampstead Lycée girl. Her daddy is the Chairman of the Bank of India. Enormously lovely girl.

Mr Stephen Chenowitz: the Montague-Jones family accountant. Gatekeeper to my trustfund. Talks about investments and fiscal reform while I swing round and round in his amazing chairs.

Lord Henry 'Hal' Coeburg: Godspeed Academy boy. Close friend of Jackdaw Penry.

Miss Elizabeth Condou: Notre Dame, Year Eleven, home tutor. Doesn't wear enough sun-block on her face.

Master Farrow Cordell: One of Kitten's on-again-off-again 'close male friends'. A regular at 'Catastrophe 13' night club.

Coutts & Co: Bank which only looks after rich people's money. When my Coutts debit card stops working I call Daddy and Daddy calls Coutts and then the card works again. It really is terribly clever.

Miss Bettina Criddlington-Shaw: One of my close friends at Hampstead Lycée. Top girl.

D

Miss Vixen Diaz-Brocklehurst: Awesome best friend, full time space-cadet, prettiest girl in Hampstead, future society It-girl.

Miss Frangipan Diaz-Brocklehurst: Vixen's older sister. Runway supermodel, specializes in swimwear.

Mrs Ramona Diaz-Brocklehurst: Vixen's mummy. Ex-Argentinian runway model specializing in swimwear.

Mr Harold 'Deathbreath' Douglas: Mathematics teacher. Obsessed with equations. Breath smells like Satan's bumcleft.

Master Stephanos Drakkakis: Kitten's close personal male friend. Greek diplomat's son. Habitual drunk driver.

Master Steel Drum: Kitten's close personal male friend. Society It-boy. Musician. Regular at Catastrophe 13. Could do with a good wash and a fogging with a pest-repellent spray.

Mr Zane Drum: Steel's father. Former lead singer with legendary 1980s electro-band Yellow Dawn. Reformed heroin addict, black belt in Aikido.

E

Miss Striker Earhart: Incredible, mega-boobed, *trés* hilarious, party-girl blonde/red/black/blue (tick as applicable) haired extraordinaire. Occasional Hampstead Lycée pupil.

Dr Paloma Earhart: Striker's mother. Cognitive Behavioural Therapist specialising in psycho-sexual disorders. Spanish. Slightly mental.

The Right Honourable Elanby-Picadelle: Prescription

medication addict (Ritalin/diazepam/viocodin). Kitten's fellow inmate at Paradise Vision. Son of Conservative MP, Lord Caius Picadelle.

G

Miss Georgina Gibbs: Daddy's personal assistant in New York. She used to be his assistant in London, but she was so good he took her with him to New York.

Mr Brandon Gissamo: A-list Hollywood actor, famous for multi-million dollar grossing movies. *Bang! Smash! Crash! Thump!* and *Bulls on a Boat*. Happily Married, apparently.

Master Sebastian Gloot: Mummy's intern who she found at St Martin's School of Art. This is the person who actually does all the interior designing.

Miss Imelda Gloringdale (RIP): Ex-Hampstead Lycée girl. Was eaten by a lion during her Gap year in Africa. Living proof that you can't have a fondu party on the Serengeti. Terribly sad.

H

Mr Harper: Archery instructor. Apparently the micro-surgeon Daddy paid for was very good and Mr Harper's face will be good as new eventually.

Miss Olivia 'Livvy' Heatherington-Sykes: Very, very funny Hampstead Lycée girl and close friend.

Mrs Pearl Highford: Mother's best friend. Lives in an

enormous farmhouse in Surrey and spends all day being photographed for flashy lifestyle mags pretending to make her own organic cheese.

Miss Jemima Highford: Pearl's daughter. Head of house at Asquith Ladies Academy. If I ever need to know how my mother thinks I should be living my life, I just look at ruddy Jemima.

Master Felix Hayes-Burlington: My oldest friend. Complete and utter legend and all round nice guy. Mummy wants me to marry Felix because 'he is of good stock' (ie: he is so rich he could buy Wales and turn it into a Rollerdisco).

Dr Henry Hayes-Burlington: Felix's daddy. The son of Jarvis J Burlington the ultra-famous author. Hates the 21st century, loves antiques, dusty piles of books and reading by candlelight.

Dr Persephone Hayes-Burlington: Felix's mummy. Professor of English Literature at University College London. Likes riding around London on a clanky bicycle wearing a cape.

The Right Honourable Petronella Hardy: Hampstead Lycée girl. Petronella would really rather prefer it if you used her title when you speak to her as she's not like everyone else, she has a title, OK? Right? Super.

K

Master Kwame Kobina: Mega-hot boy. Tall, gorgeous, clever, funny, wants to be a doctor and go to Africa and save people's lives. Sigh.

Mrs Mercy Kobina: Proud Mummy of Kwame Kobina. Says exactly whatever is going through her head.

L

Miss Karina Lugosi: One of Flash's nannies from Hungary. The hippy-dippy one who wears the mini-skirts.

M

Sir Hugh Manningford-Bowes: CEO of Globalnation Chemical Inc. Daddy's golf buddy, although their friendship has been strained since Knute handcuffed himself to him.

Mrs Maria Minsk: Our amazing housekeeper. Has been with our family so long she feels like our mummy. Sometimes I call her Mummy. My real mummy doesn't like that at all.

Mr Augustus Montague: Mummy's brother, recovered alcoholic. Only stopped drinking when he had to live in his car Don't get him chatting about it, he'll go on ALL DAY.

Mrs Jocasta Montague-Jones: My mummy. Interior

designer, party planner, trained Reiki healer. Does a terrible amount of good work for charities.

Mr James Jones: My daddy. Head honcho of Spike Global Media. Often works in New York, Moscow, Tokyo and Sydney, but that's fine as we iChat.

Master Flash Niagara Montague-Jones: My little brother. Tiny increidbly gifted evil genius.

Miss Kitten Calypso Montague-Jones: No need for an explanation.

Master Knute Hadrian Montague-Jones: My big brother. Britain's sexiest eco-warrior, according to the style magazines.

Lady Octavia Montague: Granny. Has never done a day's work in her life and is ruddy proud of it. Old-school posh.

Master Dragon Zinnah Montague-Jones (formerly known as Zinnah Obtanwu): My youngest brother. Used to live in Liberia in an orphanage. Doesn't seem too bothered about going back.

Macbeth Montague-Jones: Stupid yet loveable labrador who belongs to Knute, which doesn't explain why *I*'m always up at 5am letting it out for 'fresh air'.

Master Maxwell Moss: Godspeed Academy boy. One of Jackdaw Penry's gang.

Miss Florence Mossop-Hill: Chronic self-harmer and Paradise Vision inmate.

O

Mr Cyril Obdulu: One of mummy's drivers. Comes from Nigeria. One of the most awesome grown-ups ever. Once took Flash and I to the McDonalds Drive-thru and bought us a McFlurrywurry. Likes God and listening to BBC Radio London.

P

Mr Matthew Park: Mummy's personal assistant. Tall, handsome, clever, very patient. The poor person who has to sort Mummy's life out.

Master Jackdaw Penry: Godspeed Boys Academy, dreamy mega-hunk, or so every single girl at Hampstead Lycée thinks.

Mr Pablo Picasso: Artist – deceased. Used to date Granny in the 1950s. Did that painting of her she has in her loo where she has six boobs.

Mr Baalthazar Penry: Jackdaw's daddy. International businessman and world-famous playboy. Hangs out with Richard Branson.

Mrs Boudecia Prendergast: Headmistress of Hampstead Lycée for Young Ladies. Quite scary. Needs to lighten up a bit (not that anyone would tell her that).

S

Dr Franz Sarzberg: The family therapist. We all see Dr Sarzberg during the week to discuss our 'thoughts and feelings' and he is supposed to be sorting it all out. As yet I see no evidence.

Miss Alessandra Sabitini: Hampstead Lycée girl. Her mummy drives a mercedes and drops her off on way to yoga with her camel-toe showing through her yoga leotard. Yak!

Mr Peche Sarrasto: Winchester Boys School mega-hunk. Dated Striker Earhart (for about seven minutes).

Mr Voychek Slowikowski: One of Mummy's drivers. Used to be in the Polish military. Seems to think he still is.

Miss Amelia Strang: Hampstead Lycée girl. One of Blitzen Trapper's BFFs.

Lady Iris Stanhope-Smythe: Tiny, shy, squeaky Hampstead Lycée girl. Iris and I are sort of family as we're both related to the Queen.

Mr Singhpal: Mummy's dietician. Mummy calls him and says 'why am I fat?' and he says 'You eat too many cakes' and she screams at him and he gives her diet pills and books her in for a colonic flush out.

Shim: the man/woman who collects the tampax bins.

Lord Rufus Stanhope-Smythe: Iris's big brother. Legendary ladies man although I don't fancy him as we're kind of related. Not that this stops a lot of people. As far as I can see, most of Hampstead is sort of inbred.

T

Miss Blitzen Trapper: Most popular, wealthy girl at Hampstead Lycée. A lot of people find Blitzen a little terrifying and call her a bully, but I don't, I like her. I really do. Blitzen if you are reading this I think you are AMAZING. (Please don't hurt me).

Mr Onslow Trapper: CEO of Trapper Aerospace Inc. Blitzen's daddy. I think he owns a factory that makes aeroplanes but Flash says he makes bombs and tanks and guns. That can't be true can it?

V

Miss Rosalla Vajna: One of Flash's nannies from Hungary. The stern one who Mummy says is lazy as she keeps finding her asleep under Flash's bed.

Love Poppet? Then you'll adore Shiraz Bailey Wood. Look out for the first of her slammin' diaries

...TUESDAY – 8PM

Soapstars on Skates is on TV and our Staffy's snout is jammed up my armpit. Dad's got out the karaoke machine, Mum's setting fire to the kitchen – least that's what it smells like – and Nan has dropped off on the couch. Yeah, BORED!

But hey, Nan's got me a buff leather diary for Christmas! So now, I – Shiraz Bailey Wood – can write down all my 'goings on': hanging roundBurger King Car Park in Bezzie's Vauxhall Nova. Falling out with my hippy sister. Trying not to murder my little bruv. Definitely NOT thinking about school...

Keeping it real...

http://shirazbaileywood.bebo.com

Love Poppet? Then you'll adore Shiraz Bailey Wood. Look out for the second of her slammin' diaries

OH MY DAYS!

I've only gone and passed SEVEN GCSEs! Dad and Cava-Sue are chuffed to bits. Murphy reckons I cheated. Mum is pulling her best dog's bum face. She's not happy, I can tell ...

So, Mayflower Sixth Form here I come! Time to ditch the gold hoops and the spray tan and get myself a long scarf, some A4 folders and a new pencil case. Shiraz Bailey Wood is entering a new phase. Clever, sophisticated and definitely not skiving off ... Staying real ...

http://shirazbaileywood.bebo.com

Love Poppet? Then you'll adore Shiraz Bailey Wood. Look out for the third of her slammin' diaries

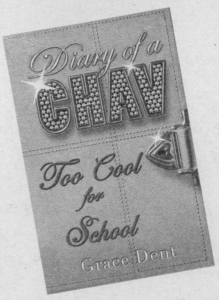

Diary of a CHAV
Too Cool for School
Grace Dent

It's all change for Shiraz Bailey Wood and Carrie Draper! We're chucking in school, we're getting jobs in London and we're leaving ESSEX FOR EVER!

Oh my days. I am PROPER excited! I'm signing up with a temping agency while I work on my 'lifeplan'. Carrie's all sorted for her place at 'Butterz Beauty School'.

I can't wait to share a flat with Carrie! And I'm taking my diary with me to write about every second of life in the big city ...

Shizza and Carrie; moving up in the world ... but ALWAYS keeping it real.

http://shirazbaileywood.bebo.com